THE SON

First published in 2013 by
Istros Books
London, United Kingdom
www.istrosbooks.com

ISBN: 978-1908236128
Printed in England by
CMP (UK) , Poole, Dorset

Education and Culture DG

Culture Programme

This project has been funded with support from the
European Commission. This publication reflects the
views only of the author, and the Commission cannot
be held responsible for any use which may be made of
the information contained therein.

THE SON

Andrej Nikolaidis

Translated from the Montenegrin by Will Firth

O how silent was the house when Father passed into the darkness.

- Georg Trakl, *Dream and Derangement*

Everyone, whatever he is and quite irrespective of what he does, is repeatedly thrown back upon his own resources, like a nightmare forced to rely on itself.

- Thomas Bernhard, *The Cellar*

I

Everything would have been different if I'd been able to control my repulsion, I realised.

The sun was still visible through the lowered blinds. It had lost all its force and now, unable to burn, it disappeared behind the green of the olive groves which extended all the way to the pebbly beach of Valdanos and on as far as Kruče and Utjeha; bays sardined with bathers determined to absorb every last carcinogenic ray before going back to their accommodation. There they would douse their burnt skin with imitations of expensive perfumes, don their most revealing attire and dash off to discos and terraces with *turbofolk* music, full of confidence that tonight they would go down on another body with third-degree burns; possessing and then forgetting another human being almost identical to themselves.

At first I'd resolved to stay in bed a bit longer, but I had to get up because the stench of sweat in the room was unbearable. The room is located on the western side of the house, and it's as hot as a foundry in there in the afternoons. The sun beats against the walls for hours and hours. Even when the bugger goes down, the walls still radiate the heat. They bombard me with it all night long. Ever since we moved into the house and I first lay in that bed, I've sweated. I wake at three in the morning and have to get out of bed because the pillow and the sheet are drenched with perspiration and start to stink. What's more, they stink dreadfully – it's simply unbearable. My own body drives me out of bed.

Making that room the bedroom was a catastrophic decision. We carried in the bed, wardrobe and bookshelves, and sealed the unhappy fate of our marriage, although we wouldn't realise it until later. Nothing could survive the night in that room, certainly nothing as fragile and bloodless as our marriage.

For two years I sweated, woke horrified by the reek of my own body and drank coffee on the balcony for hours. Shortly before dawn, I would fall asleep again briefly on the couch in the living room. Worn out by insomnia and fatigue, I would go in and cuddle her when she woke. For two years I tried to grasp what was amiss and why everything seemed to go wrong for us. I strained my mind as best I could, exhausted by insomnia and the dissatisfaction which filled the house. For two years I wasn't even able to think. And then it was all over. She left. 'I can't take this anymore', she yelled, and was gone.

That same instant I threw myself onto the bed, where even just the night before we'd said 'I love you' to each other in our ritual of hypocrisy. I was asleep before I hit the pillow. I woke bathed in sweat, as usual. *She really has gone* – that was the first thing I thought when I opened my eyes. She wasn't there anymore, but the bed still stank of me.

I got up and almost fled from the bed. I closed the door behind me, determined that nothing would ever leave that room again. I plodded to the kitchen and put on some water for coffee. Then I ran back to the room and locked the door twice just to be sure.

I thought it would be good to read something, I said to myself. It really was high time. For two whole years I hadn't read anything except the crime column in the newspaper. The only things which still interested me were crime news and books about serial killers. It was as though only overt eruptions of evil could jolt me out of my indifference. I no longer had the energy for the hermeneutics of evil. That was behind me now. I could no longer stand searching for evil in the everyday actions of so-called 'ordinary people'. Instead, I chose vulgar manifestations of evil. If a man killed thirty people and buried them under his house, that still had a wow factor for me. But I'd lost the strength to deal with the everyday animosities, suppressed desires and cheap tricks of the people I met: those who treated me as if I was blind, convinced that they've duped me into believing their good intentions and made a total fool of me, while I simply looked through them as if they didn't exist.

He Offered Himself for Dinner, the paper wrote that morning. The crime column reported on the cheerful story of Armin Meiwes, a cannibal from Germany, who had joined an online cannibal community. Humans are sociable beings: they come together when they're born, they flock together when they go off to do their military service and learn to kill other human beings, they come together to mate and to marry, and ultimately they also congregate when they want to eat one another. Meiwes had found a place where kindred souls gathered. He wanted to eat someone and confided this to his friends from the cannibal community. When he placed an announcement in the forum, replies came in from 400 people who wanted to be eaten. And so he chose one of them. It seems this fellow had particular demands: he requested that he and his benefactor celebrate a 'last supper' together and eat his penis before he be killed. Obliging Meiwes wanted to fulfil his wish, but after their initial enthusiasm they agreed that the meal was inedible. The paper then went on to explain how the 'volunteer' then felt sick and started saying the Lord's Prayer. Meiwes, whom doctors established to be quite normal, stated that he skipped the prayer because 'he couldn't decide who his father was – God or the Devil – so he didn't know whom he should be praying to'. In any case, Meiwes killed the fellow after the prayer, later ate him and filmed the whole business.

I went to the bookshelf and took down Eliot's *The Waste Land*, which a friend had given us in our first summer in the house. The November of that year was rainy and condemned us to stay at home since the continuous deluges made our walks through the olive grove impossible. That month we tried to achieve the idyll from B-movies, sitting in armchairs in *our* living room with a fire crackling in *our* fireplace. We sat and read Eliot. I read aloud and she listened. I loved her then, like I always loved her. Then I couldn't take it anymore, like I'd never been able to take it anymore.

10

But I decided to go on after all, like I always decide I should go on. Things never fail *because of* me, nor do they go off well *thanks to* me. They always happen with me as a bystander. I just adapt to them.

As a child I imagined life as an enormous desert which I had to walk through while trying not to disturb a thing or to leave any trace. Not one footprint was to remain in the sand after I was gone, not one flake of ash from the fire I laid, not one bone of an animal I killed to eat, not one scrap of waste from the caravan I met, not one tree at the oasis whose bark I carved my initials in, not one woman in a village with a child of mine by her side. I was just passing through, and I took care that no-one noticed and was able to say: he was here. That's how I thought back then, and that's how I still think today. But that's not what I did. I got married. I took a wife but continued travelling without a trace. In the end she declared 'I can't take this anymore!' and left. I could have said that too, but I didn't – she said it because she was stronger than me.

April is the cruellest month, according to Eliot. But he never lived on the Montenegrin riviera, and his fellow citizens didn't rake in wealth by renting out rooms. He never saw tourists arriving in his peaceful town like hordes of Huns and turning it into a giant, barbarian amusement park, and he never felt how it feels when your habitat shrinks to the boundaries of your courtyard, because simply leaving the house means having to forge your way through a seething mass of foreign bodies, all of whom are ugly, loud and possessed by the pursuit of pleasure. It is this that always forces me to rush back home in panic, constantly vigilant for the omnipresent, lurking danger: I return to the world of my own property, separated by a tall fence from the rest of the world which has been occupied by unknown and terrible people. August is the cruellest month, I say.

I think it was Al-Ghazali who wrote that *heaven is surrounded by suffering, whereas hell is surrounded by pleasures*. Seen from up on the forested hill where my house is, the town I live in looks like hell in the summertime. Tourism is a trade in pleasure, and people in a tourist town are indeed *surrounded by pleasures*. So Al-Ghazali was right: I am in hell because I am *surrounded by pleasures*. Sartre is also right when he says *hell is the others*. Their pleasure is my hell.

The phone rang. A friend was calling to tell me that a DVD edition of the film *Cannibal Holocaust* had just arrived from America.

'What's that?' I asked him.

'A film about an expedition of film-makers, who come across a tribe of cannibals in the Amazon jungle,' he said.

'Sounds good for starters. What happens after that?'

'Nothing much – the rest of the film is about the cannibals eating them. The distributors I got it from are called Grindhouse and specialise in the obscurest, most shocking and most repulsive films of all time,' he explained, not without enthusiasm. 'Imagine what I've just seen in their catalogue: there's a whole range of films where people are put to the most terrible of tortures, raped, slashed open, quartered and eaten. There are also titles where it says *No animals suffered in the making of this film*. Get that?' he yelled into the receiver.

'I get it,' I answered through my teeth.

'They're worried that some lovers of cannibalism, who watch movies of people being disembowelled, might feel squeamish about violence towards animals,' he bellowed.

'I'm afraid I get it,' I said.

I realised I wouldn't be able to read any more after that. There's always something at the last instant which prevents me from reading. For reading and any kind of mental exertion I need leisure. If I never felt bored, I'd never write anything. And I was still bored now, as usual, but for some time I'd been unable to think why I should read or write at all and why it was important to 'develop my mind'. I gave up all thought of reading and turned on the computer.

I couldn't get onto the internet. The dial-up connection kept tossing me offline. The telephone exchange was overloaded due to the thousands of Kosovo-born tourists who were probably sending messages to their families in Western Europe. In the summertime, these *Gastarbeiters* like to show off the pittance they've earned by insisting on these two weeks of annual holiday which bring them only frustration: no matter how much they've strutted like peacocks and seduced young girls from Peć with their gold chains and ten-year-old Mercedes, the stench of the toilets they've cleaned and will go back to clean in Munich, Stockholm or Graz still sticks in their nostrils. Now they were back from the beach and frantically phoning and sending mails, driven by the need to communicate, despite being illiterates for whom every spoken word induced suffering like that of giving birth.

I was livid with contempt and antipathy, an abhorrence which flooded over me as completely and utterly as they say saints are suffused with love. I needed to see open space: the soothing emptiness of the sea; a blue unpolluted by people. I rushed out onto the balcony.

The first shades of night were falling. The sun was setting once more behind my great-uncle's olive grove, which is what we called the hill laden with rows of overgrown olive trees. In fact, it was fifty hectares of viper- and boar-infested scrub blocking our view of the sea. My father claimed he had once seen 'something otherworldly' come down to land behind the hill. I never managed to convince him that it was just the sun. Evening after evening, we sat on the terrace waiting for darkness to fall. We watched in silence as the sun slowly disappeared behind the silhouette of the hill, which had always stood between me and the world. When the light was gone, my father would get up, state resolutely, 'No way, that wasn't the sun!' and disappear into the house. From then on, the only sign of his existence would be strains of Bach which escaped from the dark of the bedroom, where he lay paralysed by the depression which had abused him for two decades.

That evening the hill caught on fire. Instead of feeling a breeze from the sea, I was hit in the face by the heat of the burning forest. The fire would erase all my father's labours once more, I thought. After each blaze, the police scoured the terrain searching for evidence which would lead them to the culprit. Needless to say, they never found anything: not a single piece of broken glass or a match, let alone a trace of the firebug. 'They'll never find out who set fire to our hill, I tell you. How can they when the fire comes from another world?' my father repeated.

When the hill burned the first time, he saw it as a sign of God: 'My whole life had passed by without me even taking a proper look at the olive grove my uncle left me. Now there's no olive grove left – just my obligation to the land,' my father spoke with the fatalism so typical of this crazy, blighted family.

He built a fence around the entire hill. He worked his way through the charred forest step by step, breaking stones and driving hawthorn-wood stakes into the rock, as if into the heart of a vampire. Then he tied barbed wire to the stakes, which tore into the flesh of his hands. For months he came home black from head to toe like a coal miner who had just emerged from the deepest pit. And that's what he was: a miner. He delved into the heart of his memories. He wasn't clearing the charcoaled forest but digging at what was inside him, breaking the boulder which oppressed him, shovelling away the scree which had buried him alive. He came home all wet and sooty for months, until one day he announced that his work was done. The property was fenced in and cleared. He had built new dry stone walls and planted olive saplings. He took me and my mother onto the terrace and showed us my great-uncle's olive grove for the umpteenth time. 'I've resurrected it from the flames,' my father pronounced.

When the hill burned the second time, he installed a new fence and planted the olive trees again. As if that was not enough work, he also built a barn. Then he brought in goats from Austria. His diligence went so far that he even minded them. That year he was a goatherd. During the day he would roam over the hill with the goats; in the early evening he would bring them back to the barn for the night. 'The pasture is excellent this year –,' he said, 'fresh growth is coming up from the scorched earth, and so the goats are eating the best food. Now they're fenced in, safe from the jackals, and have a nice dry place to sleep: like a five-star hotel,' he was fond of adding.

My mother thought she knew the root of my father's devotion to the goats. She claimed to remember from my grandmother's stories that my great-uncle had tuberculosis. 'He died of it in the end, too, but he owed the last years of his life to the goats,' my mother said. 'A goatkeeper came from Šestani and brought him milk. He lived on even after the doctors had written him off, thanks to that milk. He had no wife or children, only your grandmother – the wife of his deceased brother, your father, and those goats up in Šestani. He lived with your grandmother and your father, and the goats helped him survive,' my mother told me.

Born in the coastal range of Crmnica, my great-uncle had left for America in his youth. He fled his impoverished village for New York, only to go hungry in the big city for the next three years. He slept in neglected warehouses and stole vegetables from the markets to feed himself. Occasionally he would kill a stray dog, and then he thanked the Lord for the skills with knife and stick he had learnt hunting birds on Lake Skadar. 'After the first week I knew I'd succeed. I knew I'd survive,' he later told his brother's wife and her son. 'I eked out a lonely living in the middle of New York as if I was up in the wilds of Montenegro.' The boy stared, riveted, while he spoke about the dog skin he had made shoes from. The boy had never seen his own father, but he imagined he must have looked like this uncle with the short, grizzled moustache who now came into their kitchen in shoes of strong-smelling leather (maybe even dog-leather?), hugged his mother and him, slipped some money for sweets into his pocket like uncles do, and in the evening told them tales of his adventures. What an uncle, what a man!

He made it good in America but died of a broken heart, my grandmother told my father, who later told me: 'He never married and therefore died unhappy. "Everything I've done and all the roads I've travelled have been in vain because I'm dying without a son", he said before he died.' My mother, while she was alive, maintained he would have lived longer if he'd stayed in America: 'But he came back, saw your father and fretted for the son he'd never had – that's what killed him in the end.'

He slaved away all his life, only to die in misery. But he left all his worldly goods to his sister-in-law. That saved her from the penury she faced after her husband's death and would have had to raise her child in. 'All my young years I ate the fruits of my uncle's labour; I fed on his sweat and suffering,' my father used to say.

The man from Crmnica laboured, suffered and died. That's the whole story about each and every one of us: the complete biography of the human race. He was buried fifty years ago, and what's left of him is going up in flames tonight.

Now it's all over, I thought as I watched the flames rising into the night sky. The hill was burning for the third time in ten years. The fire would be my father's final defeat. He no longer had the strength to raise the property from the ashes again. After my mother died, the enforced loneliness he was ill-prepared for exacerbated his depression. He hardly ever left the house anymore. He would just sit in the darkened living room all day. I asked myself what he was thinking about, but in fact I didn't really care. I just hoped he *was* thinking and that at least his thoughts might manage to break through the tall, smooth walls of depression which surrounded him.

That night the hill was on fire, but he didn't go out in front of the house even to watch the flames which were swallowing up all his labours. From the balcony of my house I watched his terrace, without hope that he would appear or maybe even step through the door he had decided to die behind. His wife had died, and mine had left me. Two men, each in his own house, whom not even a fire blazing a hundred yards away could unite; not even to watch the spectacle of it devouring their property.

The burning hill sounded like the crackle of an old record. Or the hiss of a cassette. Something you could get rid of by pressing the Dolby button. But now the flames spread out of control down the slopes of the hill. I turned on the local radio and learnt that the first houses had been evacuated. Behind the first houses, of course, were more houses. And then mine. I was horrified by the thought that the whole neighbourhood had again pooled its efforts and was doing its utmost to stop the fire, and in doing so was obstructing the fire brigade in doing its job. I could just imagine the neighbours gossiping about me. 'He's the only one who's not here,' I could hear them whisper to each other. 'It's their property that's burning and he's not here. Why do we have to put out their fire?' they asked themselves, ignoring the fact that they were out there protecting their own houses, not my olive grove. They were only fighting the fire in my olive grove because they feared it could encroach on their houses. 'My olive grove' wasn't mine anyway.

They said on the radio that the government had sold all its Canadair aircraft to Croatia because it had assessed that the country didn't need a fleet of water bombers. That was in the springtime. The coastal area had been set alight in the first days of June and was still

19

burning – from Lastva above Tivat to Budva, Petrovac, Možura and all the way to Lake Skadar. Now Ulcinj was ablaze too: the flames had spread from my great-uncle's hill to the first houses in the suburb of Liman. The walls of the Old Town were also at risk, the radio reported.

Since the government had sold the aeroplanes, the fire was being fought with helicopters. They were hauling up water in what looked like sacks and dropping it on the fire. The instant the water fell on the ground, smoke and steam obscured its elemental beauty. Everything vanished momentarily in grey, but the flames only needed another minute or two to re-establish their reign over my father's property.

I soon tired of the scene. Three helicopters were now in operation, and it was plain to see that they would defeat the fire in what would be one more triumph of technology. Once technology and nature were pitted against each other in this way I felt there was nothing left for me. And yet I simply couldn't make up my mind as to which was more monstrous: nature itself or the methods people employ in order to dominate it. Before turning and going back into the room, I glanced over to my father's house. The lights were off, but I knew he wasn't asleep.

It was at that point that I heard the bleating of goats. The neighbour must have been herding a flock along the road towards the house. 'Eh, mate!' I heard him call, and that sound made the blood freeze in my veins. I wasn't prepared for a conversation with him. I wasn't in the state of mind to thank him for saving my father's goats from the fire, or to invite him in for a drink and have a good talk like good neighbours and real men are supposed to.

But he was already standing at the gate, which I always kept locked, and waving to me. Great: now there was no escape. I put on my boxers and went down to open up for him.

'What a tragedy, eh mate?' he droned. Fortunately he didn't expect me to answer. As he drove the goats in through the gate he continued: 'Everything your father did has burnt down. I only just managed to save these ones here. I got them out when the barn caught fire. There was no saving it. Such a great shame, ain't it mate? But that's life for you – people slave away, and sometimes you wonder what for. You slog and sweat, and then everything goes up in smoke in a flash. *It was destroyed by the flames*, they say. But it wasn't the flames – it was God.'

With this kind of attitude, he was bound to be considered a wise man by those who knew him.

Finally all the goats were in the courtyard, and I realised I was already sick of the situation. The goats themselves immediately set about what they do best: surviving. These creatures, which had only just eluded death, now grazed indifferently and stank to high heaven. The billy goats were the most accomplished in that; they stank even worse than my neighbour, who doggedly came up behind me every time I tried to move away from him to get a breath of fresh air.

'You know, old son –,' he schmoozed, determined to

get some reward for his good deed, 'I always tell people there's no better *rakija* than yours.'

'Let's go upstairs,' I said, too weak to fight against the kind of incivility where people invite themselves into others' houses.

But I hadn't set one foot on the stairs when I was compelled to turn around abruptly, feeling as if someone was watching me. And sure enough, my paranoia was justified once again: the black he-goat was looking at me intently. His yellow eyes were staring at me in the dark. Their slit-shaped pupils looked like cracks in the earth, ready to swallow me up. He threateningly flared his nostrils, from where a gleaming trail of saliva trickled. His sharp little teeth chewed the grass I'd just walked on, and he kept his eyes on me. I was sure we were thinking about the same thing: he about how to eat me, and me about my flesh disappearing into his mouth, his teeth sinking into my body and tearing off piece after piece.

'You all right, mate?' I heard the man say behind me. I turned back and saw my neighbour, whom I'd completely forgotten. For the first time in my life I was glad to see him. For the first time I found comfort in another human being, despite his gap-toothed smile and half-witted gaze set beneath a low brow and red lop-ears. *Away, away from the animals!* I thought as I rushed up the stairs. My neighbour ran after me in surprise.

'Whoa, easy does it, mate. You look a bit pale,' I heard him say.

I led him into the house and cast one more glance at

the he-goat. He was still standing in the same place and staring at me. It was as if he wanted to make it clear to me that I'd opened the gate of my house for him, that he'd entered and that he'd never leave. He'd stand there and wait for me until the end, whenever my end would be.

'I don't have any *rakija*. Do you drink whisky?'

'I drink everything,' he said.

I poured myself a full glass and just two fingers for him because I wanted him to leave as soon as possible. We sat in the armchairs in the living room, opposite each other. I put the bottle down on the table between us, hoping it would obstruct my view of him, but it was in vain: the table was too low and the bottle too small.

Through the balcony door, I could see the tips of the flames. They must have been frazzling what was left of the hill. Yet I found comfort in the flames. They were the perfect excuse for me not to look at the fellow in front of me. He'd think I was fretting because of the fire or that I felt sorry for my father. He tried to start a conversation but soon gave up and decided to leave me to my sorrow.

'I'll pour myself, mate, don't you mind. You just go ahead and think,' he reassured me.

After that we sat in silence. When he'd quaffed all my whisky and my neck was stiff from looking out through the balcony door, he left. As he was going, he said: 'You're a good man.' I nodded, refusing to look at him. When he closed the door behind him, I burst into tears.

That's how *she* cried, too, as if she was imploring

someone. And that someone was *me*, I sometimes thought, and yet it was as if she was beseeching someone who wouldn't hear. The only purpose of crying is self-pity, which brings us the greatest satisfaction – a wet orgasm after emotional masturbation. We pity ourselves because there's no-one else who would. Self-pity is held in great stead. Only someone who cries and weeps convulsively over themselves can hope to gain the sympathy of others. But it only lasts an instant. Everyone turns back to themselves in a flash because people are only capable of ongoing agony in relation to themselves. And who can blame them: being alive is an unquestionably tragic fact which can induce nothing but tears.

When she finally stopped sobbing, she left me. All at once she wiped away her tears, and instead of a tearful glance she sent me one full of hate.

'You've destroyed me. I curse every day of our life together,' she snarled.

I saw clearly where this was heading. Two or three sentences more and she'd say I'd made her want to die, I thought. But she didn't.

'Life with you was hell,' she said instead, 'a hell I'm now leaving. I'm going to start life again. On second thought, I should be grateful to you because you've aroused the desire for life in me again: a life after you. Now I know there's a life after death.' She laughed hysterically. 'Life *after you*. Thank you for everything,' she shouted as she threw her things into her suitcase.

She left before I could say anything in return. I simply

stood in the hall, staring at the door she'd slammed behind her, left alone in the house which until just a moment ago had been our home. What did I expect? That the door would open again, that she would come in, laugh her golden laugh and once more grace this damned house with her smile; with the smile which made me fall in love with her in the first place; the smile I married? It was only this morning that she left me, yet I can no longer remember the reason why. What happened between us? What was it that became so unbearable? I thought about her but couldn't come up with a single reason why she found me so abhorrent, nor of how I'd become estranged from her, incapable of living close together. I knew now that I loved her. I thought about her smile and loved it like the very first day I met her, and it seemed as if nothing untoward had happened at all, nothing had changed. I realised that her leaving had brought everything full circle: she had gone and everything returned to nothing.

I remembered watching her singing in the kitchen in the immaculate light which came in through the open window, like the illumination in baroque paintings. She stood there like an angel with wings outspread, too tender for this world. It seemed only a moment before her mangled, fragile form would float heavenward and her wings would fall into the mire in which I reside. But then she started singing, and the terrible dissonance destroyed the picture.

'Darling, you look like an angel but sing like a toad,' I told her.

As a matter of fact, everyone becomes unbearable once we get to know them a little better. That's why the most beautiful women are those on painters' canvases, where they're limited to their appearance. Beautiful they are, and that's all we need to know about them. Because any other detail about their biographies, habits and thoughts would repulse us and turn delight into disgust. I can just imagine how the girl with the pearl earring must have stunk. Europe at that time didn't have bathrooms, so it's hard to think of European women of that era as anything other than carriers of the plague bacillus. This woman, as we know, was a maidservant. Before she sat for the painter determined to immortalise her beauty, in other words the lie about her, she must already have cooked the main meal, scrubbed the floors and done all the shopping. She's sure to have worked up a sweat at least three times, and being in the same room as her must have been awful. But there's not a man alive who doesn't desire to kiss her when he sees her on a museum wall.

Art always lies, as a matter of fact. It seduces us with its lies like a killer seduces a girl standing in the rain in front of the school and waiting for her mother, who's running late because her lover needed several minutes longer to reach orgasm that day. It takes us by the hand just as that girl is, blinded by lies, and leads us away from the truth, away from life. Art creates the impression that things have meaning and always happen for a reason, but the truth is different, of course: we never find out why, nor do we perceive the meaning of what happens to us.

Things are neither beautiful nor justifiable. They simply stink like the sweaty body of Jesus did up on the cross, or the masses who tried to stone him and the disciples who bewailed him; they stink like the saints and sinners, the convicted and the executioners, da Vinci's *Mona Lisa* and Vermeer's *Girl with a Pearl Earring*, and especially van Gogh's shoes, which Heidegger, amid the stench of beer and sausages, claimed to be those of a peasant. We, the living, stink too; we wash in vain because filth, not cleanliness, is our natural state. We clean ourselves but always get dirty again. And we stink hideously: from the day we're born until our dying day, and even after we're dead. We stink *in both life and death*.

Only now that she's gone can she be beautiful again, and only now am I able to love her again. Because now I'm forgetting all I had learnt about her, and can allow only her beauty to remain. Her smiling face. I will cherish that image just as precious paintings are stored in high-security museums.

Apropos women ... I heaved myself out of the armchair and sat again at the computer. I connected to the internet at the first attempt and typed *'free cumshot pics'* into the search engine. It came up with 40 million porno sites, and I chose one at random. I saved several women's faces to my desktop. Splattered with sperm, they stared up adoringly at the studs who'd just ejaculated on them as if they were pagan fertility gods. Cumshots are my favourite segment of pornography: the wanton spilling of seed, the defiant and futile squandering of fatherhood.

Ready to masturbate, I thought! After all, masturbation is the ultimate consequence of the Cartesian concept of the *subject*. I gazed at the image on the screen: a siliconed Korean knelt in front of a circumcised black. Talk about multicultural. Political correctness is only tolerable in pornography, I thought – this is its true place. Because what is political correctness if not a pornography of correctness?

But it wasn't to be; this happens to me all the time. My masturbation has become excessively intellectual and too discursive for it to be possible. For months I've been unable to feel sexual arousal and instead resort to fulfilling a need to deconstruct porno images, can you believe it? My own hunger for the grotesque will destroy me, I yelled, pacing round and round. It was clear that my need to discover the grotesque in every detail would be the end of me: I look at everything with contempt because I see discord and misery in it all. Yet the only alternative to repulsion is compassion, which is equally lethal. In the end I'll die, and when they've buried me everyone will hold me in contempt. There will be no-one to mourn for me.

'It's unbearable how my brain works!' I roared.

Going out onto the balcony, I gripped the railing with both hands.

'I can't take this repulsion anymore,' I cried, 'no-one would be able to. But what can I do when I keep seeing all those things, when the wretchedness and filth drive me to disgust and pity, and when they crucify me like Christ. I'm like Christ on the cross, who instead of love for the mob who stoned him feels only disgust. And the stinker who cuffed Christ while he was carrying the cross: what if Jesus saw in him only a wretch who'd found out the day before that his wife was cheating him, and who hit him today because he didn't slap her yesterday? What if that's how it was? What if Christ simply loathed him? What if he laughed at those grotesque creatures and then breathed his last, adrift in the ocean of sorrow which washed over him, sorrow because of all the misery on Earth. What if that's how it was? Everything would go down the plughole and there would be nothing but agony, like everything really has gone down the plughole and my life is nothing but agony. Death is the only fact which one can build optimism on – only death can finally bring hope…'

I stood on the balcony, howling out this tirade, and then stopped myself when I suddenly remembered my father. The terrible thought that I might waken him forced me into silence. I glanced over to his house, but he hadn't turned on the light or come out onto the terrace. He hadn't heard me, after all. I had avoided that reproachful question, 'What are you doing, for goodness' sake?'; that question which I had always found the most shameful and frustrating. Once again there was no sign of my father. I tried to recall when I'd last seen him, but I couldn't quite remember: I now wondered if he left the house at all anymore.

If *I* don't wake him, the dogs butchering each other down on the road will, I thought. A huge black tyke was tearing away at an unfortunate hunting dog. And a whole pack of dirty mutts and mongrels had come bolting up behind; canine freaks combining all the worst features of their forebears. The black tyke seized the slender hunting dog by the neck, immediately drawing blood and maddening the black leader's entourage – that incestuous, degenerate pack. The long-bodied dog died in agony as dozens of jaws rent at it, pulled at its limbs and tore it apart on the sticky, hot asphalt. That will wake my father, I thought, and everything will end in a row, like every other conversation we've had since my mother died: without her standing between us as both dyke and bridge. Without her, our relationship was finally reduced to its very essence of mutual antipathy. My father had grated on my nerves even when I was a child, when I would be annoyed by everything he said or did. The trauma I carry with me from my earliest years is my father. I must have had a hundred nervous breakdowns in my childhood, and each of them because of him. Every time my father thought of giving me a goodnight kiss, of coming into my room, stroking my hair and saying something to me which *he* thought was affectionate – *he* who never learnt anything about children, who never learnt to live with his child, who never really accepted the fact that he had a child ... Every time he stroked my hair and kissed me on the neck after his 'affectionate' and fortunately brief monologue...

He even kissed me that evening after Milan had fallen from the gnarled, enchanted, 500-year-old maple. They said it was me who had talked him into climbing it. I don't remember that, and I don't know why Milan climbed the tree that particular day, like I know he had many times before. Perhaps he climbed it to needlessly prove to me once again that he was the elder brother, and thus braver and stronger. It turned out that a man was hoeing around the olive trees on the property next door: he heard our argument and me telling Milan that I hated him and demanding that he climb the tree all the way to the top. Milan refused because it had rained and the bark was wet, and then the man heard me saying I would climb it instead. Soon there came a scream and the sickening sound of a bone breaking.

The body of his seven-year-old son was at the city mortuary in Bar that time my father leaned over my bed, covering me with the bridge of his body, and said, 'Don't cry, we love you.' I listened to his steps receding, heard my mother's sobs and the door of their room close. It closed once and for all for me. From that moment on, it was no longer the long hall and the two doors which separated us. Between us lay dead Milan, the blood trickling from his small, fractured skull and being borne away by the water from the old Turkish drinking fountain. From that moment on, we were separated by my guilt. My father never said that to me. He didn't have to: it was enough for him just to look at me, or even worse, to kiss me. Every evening I awaited my punishment, but it never came. Instead there was the *goodnight kiss*. Only today do I realise how cruelly I was punished – that kiss was the punishment. I was 'forgiven', and it had been 'decided' that Milan's death would never be mentioned in front of me. I was left to take care of my punishment myself. They could just as well have said: We won't mention it but we know it was your fault, just as you know it was your fault.

Every time my father kissed me I cried hysterically, spat into my palm and tried to rub clean the place on my skin he'd kissed; the spot he'd blemished with his lips, which in the very act of forgiveness spoke: *It was your fault*. That kiss was an imprint on my skin, a mark branded into me every evening. Those who forgive us are our harshest judges. I clenched the bedcover with my teeth, pummelled the mattress with my feet and cried into the pillow. For hours and hours. In the end I'd drift off to sleep in the oblivion which came with the exhaustion of my young body. Fatigue finally brought salutary bluntness to my mind and senses. First my father and every thought of him would disappear; then the door which had unsuccessfully tried to protect me from his coming; and after that there would no longer be the room or the bed. Nothing any more, and no-one.

The lights in his house didn't go on. I feared he might come out onto the terrace and that I would soon hear the creak of his gate and his fast steps as he stormed towards my house, ready to give me yet another telling-off.

***

My mother cursed the day she bore me. She was in hospital in Podgorica, melting away before my eyes as uterine cancer ate her up from the inside; she literally dematerialised as the emptiness of her womb spread like the expanding universe, and she disappeared into that void like light is devoured by a black hole. And as she lay there dwindling away, she told me that although she was dying, it was with the greatest happiness, because she wouldn't have to see me or my father anymore. After being *condemned to an existence with us,* now at the end she'd at least be able to *unexist without us.* Those were her words. What surprised me most about them was that my mother had never had the slightest inclination towards philosophy. I'd never have thought that her last words would be an attempt to philosophically review her life just as it was about to be snuffed out. That amazed me, although my amazement was actually out of place. With sufficient suffering, everyone is capable of relatively accurate philosophical perception, at least as regards their own suffering. It's a fact that suffering makes people wiser, just as happiness stupefies them. And after the amount of suffering my father and I inflicted on my mother, one could actually have expected something even more philosophically profound and weighty. Yet the end result was certainly an achievement: you can't get much deeper than the insight into the solace of death, than the realisation of dying in joy.

My mother only gave up on us at the very end. Right up to her last breath she tried to reconcile my father and me, to find a way for the two of us to love each other.

She gave us her all. She gave herself up for our hatred, and we consumed her. We ate her up from the inside, from the womb which he, the father, had penetrated, and I, the son, had fled. But flee as I did, my father still entered me. I fled from the womb straight into a life where my father terrorised us not only from without but also from within.

A father manages this feat because, over time, we recognise him *in ourselves*. We realise to our horror that what we fear most – the father – is already deep inside us. We spend our whole life fleeing from the father figure but never really manage to escape, not even when he's dead. In the end we die, hoping that death will grant us release from him.

The agony of my mother's life was even greater because she ran towards death while fleeing from both husband and son; from the torture that both of us inflicted on her. But I've decided not to end up like her. I've expelled him from my life. I've driven him into his house and left him to books and Bach. I've left him to his depression. That was the only way for me to survive: *to be by myself, without him.*

Yet my mother never seemed to tire in the peace negotiations she brokered, shuttling back and forth between my father and me in what she termed an attempt to kindle love between father and son. Truces were made, only to be broken the very next day, for the most part unintentionally. The antipathy was simply too strong for her sacrifice to be like a restraining dyke, and too broad for her to bridge it. I only have the two of you, she would say, and I'd give my life to see you happy and getting along together. Only at the very end, when they had her put in a hospital bed and it became clear she'd never leave it alive, did she realise that her lifelong sacrifice had been futile. At that point, she felt thwarted and cheated, and was filled with the desire for revenge. And since my father wasn't available, she took it out on me. She called me close, conspiratorially, with her gaze riveted to the door lest someone barge into the room and foil her little plan. When I put my head against her chest to try to hear what she was whispering, she demanded that I kill her.

'Put me out of my misery, don't let me suffer like this any longer,' she murmured. 'All my life I was against euthanasia, but now I realise how stupid I was. It's my only choice now. You're my son, you have to do this for your mother.'

Her words were urgent, and she seized my head in her hands.

'Be a man. I've never asked anything of you before, but this is different. Be a man at least this once and have pity on your own mother.'

I tried to explain to her rationally and, to my mind, almost affectionately, as if speaking to a retarded child, that I couldn't do anything of the kind.

'You know I've never accepted *such* responsibility. I never have and never will,' I told her. 'You've had your whole life to kill yourself and put yourself out of your misery. You've had cancer for two years now, knowing that you're going to die in terrible pain. But instead of taking care of things yourself, you've waited until the pain is unbearable.' I was yelling at her now. 'You just sat and waited, and now you heap it all on me. Suddenly I'm the one who has to decide about life and death – me, someone who avoids obligation at all costs, refuses to influence people's lives and has just one ambition: to go unnoticed. Now I'm supposed to destroy my life because you didn't dare to put an end to yours. You didn't have the courage to end your life of misery, and instead you've decided to make mine even more miserable,' I screamed.

I stopped talking when I saw the tears in her eyes. She sobbed loudly. Her crying stabbed into my brain like long, hot nails.

I realised that I'd managed to offend her again just before her death, just when she was weakest, when actually I pitied her. I'd offended her and riddled her with venomous words, when my intentions were to say something affectionate and comforting.

But like a mortally wounded beast, she decided to bite once more. She cursed the day she bore me. Naturally, this could in no way upset me, because I also curse the day she bore me. I told her that, too, considering sincerity a virtue and holding that an upstanding person wouldn't lie to their mother in the hour of her death.

'Get out and at least leave me to die in peace,' she shrieked through her tears. That brought in the doctors, who as usual were hovering about the hospital corridors all day, ready to swoop down like vultures when they hear the cries of the dying.

All at once the room was aflutter with those white-coated scavengers, along with nurses stinking of nicotine. My mother asked them to throw me out of the room. This was just what they'd been waiting for; I'd obviously been getting on their nerves to such an extent that they despised me. So I sat out in the corridor until evening and whiled away the time by watching the goings-on in that brothel. People die in its rooms, pervaded by despair and fear, while its corridors are awash with lust and greed; with doctors lining their pockets and nurses supplementing their marital sex life. It was unbearable to see all the loathsome things which go on there, the common bribes and adulteries so familiar to anyone who has ever waited in a hospital corridor. I expected my mother to make the last sacrifice for me and save me from those insufferable scenes; to die as quickly as possible and spare me the obligation of waiting for word of her death in that disgusting corridor. My mother didn't betray me this time either: she died before evening. I tried to enter the room to give her a farewell kiss on the forehead, but the doctor said that before her death she'd expressly forbidden me from coming anywhere near her. I wasn't to touch her at all, he told me with a malicious grin.

She said that despite the fact that I was the only one who'd been with her as she lay dying. My father didn't visit her once in the whole time she was ill. He just sat riveted by depression to the armchair. He didn't even get up from the chair the day I buried Mother, leaving just myself and the two cemetery workers standing beside the grave. I didn't inform anyone about Mother's death. I didn't have an obituary notice printed, and of course I didn't permit the outrageous perversion of announcing her death in the newspaper. I had her buried in the town of Bar, where we knew no-one. That way I could be sure that nobody would come to the funeral and spoil things.

I paid the workers well. They misunderstood the gesture and considered it their duty to pretend to be deeply touched by her death. When we'd buried her I couldn't make them leave the grave. They just stood there, crossing themselves ceaselessly in compensation for the lack of mourners. 'The poor woman. To die so alone and for no-one to come to the burial...,' one lamented. 'May the dark earth rest lightly on her after such martyrdom,' the other said. I desperately wanted to be alone but they refused to go. Instead, they came up with new and ever more pathetic folkloric creations. This introduced an element of the ridiculous, which was superfluous because funerals are ridiculous as they are, in common with all situations where people feel obliged to be serious and dignified. I was reminded once again that the nicest thing we can say about a person is that one day they will die and cease to bother us. In the end I had to pay the workers double before they finally agreed to leave.

At a cemetery, surrounded by the dead, we're at the source of cognisance. At a cemetery we learn at first glance all we need to know about life – that we're going to die. I sat down on the dry stone wall by my mother's grave and lit a cigarette.

The wind blew several snowflakes into my face. I looked around and saw that I was alone at the cemetery, which extended out to all four corners of the world. Row upon row of stone crosses marched to the horizon, where threatening black clouds were mustering. War is the father of all things, I thought: an army of the dead against a heavenly army. Thunder rumbled through the valley. Both the cemetery and I witnessed those sound effects of nature in impassive silence. Wherever I looked, I saw graves mounted with crosses, upright and dignified, marking lives spent in humiliation and submission.

All around me, as far as the eye could see, stretched the future.

II

I realised I would have to leave the house as soon as possible. It was still out of the question for me to enter the bedroom and so I left it locked. But since the wardrobe containing my clothes was in there, that restricted my choice of attire for the night. I decided that anything would do and opted for the white linen suit hanging in the hall. True, I knew it would make me look like a pimp, but I considered that persona quite appropriate for a writer. Because what do writers do if not pimp out their life to lustful readers? They always write about themselves whether they want to or not, just as they're always occupied with themselves, whatever they do. To be a writer therefore means to pimp oneself, which is a perfect, self-sufficient form of prostitution, integrating both the pimp and the whore – both the marketing and the finished product.

So there I was, dressed up in the white suit and walking along the road past my father's house. I thought I could hear Bach playing inside but I wasn't sure because an easterly breeze was shaking the tops of the olive trees. Their murmur merged with the ever-present din of the crickets, making the summer evening a wall of sound. Then I was down on the road, in the shine of the street light which was working for a change. And finally I found myself in the car, and the engine of my SUV rumbled as I flipped through the CDs in the glovebox, searching for Sonic Youth and their *Song for Karen*.

Uncle's hill was still burning and the fire brigade was busy. They had parked their ridiculous red truck in the middle of the road, forcing me to squeeze between it and the illegally parked patrol car the police had arrived in. They'd come to ensure order in our suburb during the fire, but as usual they caused even greater chaos. My neighbours were there too, of course, with their emaciated cows, their scrawny, mangy dogs, and their children, who were the most undernourished and grubby of all. On top of that, these offspring were thick-headed, full of juvenile gazes which exuded a blend of primitivism and prurience – that most dangerous of all pernicious combinations of human characteristics. The adults, cows, dogs and this dubious brood were all milling around on the road, all of them equally incoherent in expressing their fear of the fire which seemed to blaze more brightly the more the fire brigade endeavoured to put it out. They all held their heads in desperation, mooed, thrashed their tails, wailed and barked. Every living thing becomes unbearably sordid the moment it fears for its life. And, as a rule, those who count for least are most afraid. There's no pitiful human being who won't make a drama out of their death if they find out they're incurably ill. Everyone around them will immediately be informed of their misfortune and will even be expected to show sympathy. In keeping with the old *friend-in-need-is-a-friend-indeed* truism, I saw that my neighbours' relatives were starting to arrive too; people whose only thought was how fortunate they were that their own house wasn't on fire. The relatives shook their heads in fake concern and consoled the wretches who were preoccupied with their bad luck and the forest igniting right next to their house.

There I was, hurriedly departing that Golgotha of human dignity. *Tunic, Song for Karen* – an awesome piece of white noise about death – blared from the car as I drove down into town. And there I was, thinking how diligent the pyromaniacs had been that night: the rubbish containers were ablaze all along the street. Like torches on the wall of a cave they illuminated the main thoroughfare leading down to the centre of unbridled touristic repulsiveness.

But I didn't get far. There was a commotion like a mass-meeting in front of the mosque which forced me to park the car and continue on foot. I literally had to struggle through the crowd. So many people could only have gathered because of a fatality, I thought. Maybe the muezzin had fallen from the minaret. Perhaps he was taken out by a man with a rifle who, after a gruelling and stressful day, was just trying to get to sleep when he started bawling his *Allahu akbar*. Or maybe he'd woken someone who'd just fallen asleep, an irascible man who was already at wits' end without the muezzin's holy droning – a walking time bomb who could explode at any moment. Yes, that's probably what happened; the muezzin called a bullet instead of the believers. The transcendental can be irritating, I mused, especially when it comes unwanted. But that supposition proved to be wrong: no-one had killed the muezzin. Instead, it turned out that a son had killed his father, after doing in his mother and brother too.

What incredible things you hear if you only mix with the crowd! Impelled by curiosity, I joined the mob in front of the mosque. People whispered about a crime they said was terrible and 'unprecedented', while I thought that an unprecedented crime would truly be something new. It would be hard to add an unwritten chapter to the comprehensive history of crime. Surely everything has been written about already, and all that happens from then on is just the perpetual repetition of the same code of crime.

'A father killing his son is sort of imaginable, but this?' people repeated in their astonishment. Those good folk of Ulcinj were ill-informed: patricide is a reinforcing bar in the foundations of this world. Sometimes it is symbolic, but sometimes people – particularly those of modest intellect – resort to literal patricide. 'Can you believe it? Such a peaceful family, who'd have thought!' People's comments reminded me of the crime reports in our daily papers, every single one of which ended with the sentence: 'The neighbours are shocked by the crime. The murderer and the victims were a harmonious family, to all appearances, and there had been nothing to herald this tragedy.' If asked, people are always stunned when a crime occurs, even one as commonplace as patricide, which every adult has committed in their infantile mind, while those who haven't yet broken free of the deadly embrace of the father commit it later. There's no family in this world which cannot be the scene of the most terrible murder. As long as they live, parents destroy their children, and their children pay them back for it and don't relinquish their thirst for vengeance until they've sent their parents to the grave. Every family home can turn into a slaughterhouse. A tiny catalyst of just a single word is often all it takes for the history of abuse and hatred, hidden under a semblance of harmony and love like in an old-fashioned memento chest, to end in bloodshed.

And yet, although a variation on a well-known theme – an evergreen crime, so to speak – this murder was interesting in its own right. The murdered father had been *a lovely man*, people said: a retiring, pious man who minded his own business. 'He never did anyone any harm, and look what happened to him,' a voice called from the crowd. The others agreed, while I was hoping that the fellow would soon finish his tribute to the deceased and move on to the gory details. After all, that's why we find murders interesting.

The son was an absolute no-gooder, they said. It had been clear from an early age that he'd be a reprobate. But his father, that *lovely man*, was eternally forgiving. 'Don't underestimate the power of forgiveness,' he told his friends, who believed in the power of punishment. To my mind, his downfall was caused by him preferring forgiveness to corporal punishment. The boy stole. Whatever he could swipe from the neighbour's garden and whatever he could stick into his pockets at the market, he took it. And then there was grandma's jewellery, grandfather's antique pistol and his cousin's bike. He even stole when he knew he'd be found out and punished. They say his mother died of shame. They caught him pickpocketing the mourners at her funeral. Over time, the neighbourhood began to blame him for every single burglary. Not that they were far wrong: their suspicions were justified most of the time. But occasionally they'd accuse him of things he hadn't done, just enough for him to become acquainted with injustice and to realise that no-one has a monopoly on it – you constantly inflict injustice on others, and they constantly inflict it on you.

There would be a furious banging on the gate of their house, interrupting the father's afternoon rest. Roused from sleep, he would go out in his striped pyjamas and wearing a hairnet which he refused to go to bed without, even if he was dead sick. The irate 'visitor' would proceed to shower him with a tirade of abuse. 'Do please calm down, Mr Karić, we'll sort it all out,' the father repeated. As he led the 'guest' into the house, he'd glance up at the first-floor window and see his son peering down into the courtyard through the curtains. When their eyes met, the father would smile, letting his son know that he forgave him and would take the blame for everything himself. The boy would run into the hall, and time and time again he heard his father enduring insults and excusing his son's escapades, which had long since grown into full-blown scandals. The yob and the rake in him came out ever stronger. When he turned twenty, old Karić the neighbour yelled at his father in the kitchen just like he had ten years earlier when the boy had broken the apple tree he'd climbed to steal the fruit. Now the boy had got Karić's daughter pregnant.

His father had sorted things out in the past, and he knew he'd sort them out now, too. After showing Karić out, the father went up to his son's room and gave him a homily which was supposed to be soul-stirring. He spoke about the power of love and forgiveness and appealed to the debt of responsibility we have towards others. After this sermon, which was futile and thus tragic, he kissed his son on both cheeks and went to the mosque, bowed with sorrow as if he bore it on his back. His son must have thought it would be the same story that day when old Karić dashed to their house and demanded that he marry his daughter.

All this I gleaned from the flurry of anecdotes about the son who killed his father, which partly stemmed from memory and were partly dreamed up by people as they went to read the green obituary notice on the wall of the mosque. The son had promised his father that he'd marry the girl, people said, but that was another lie: one day before the wedding he'd fled to America. His father reached him in New York, where he was working in a restaurant run by a compatriot, and told him he had to come home because the girl was pregnant and would soon be giving birth. She hadn't had an abortion because he couldn't countenance such a sin. The girl kept the child because the father promised Karić his son would return and marry her. But his son hung up and fled to the other end of America, even farther away from the past. He even made it as far as Los Angeles, only to receive word there that the girl had given birth to a son and, after leaving hospital, had drowned herself and the baby in Bojana River. In order to avenge the disgrace brought upon his family, old Karić went down to the quay that night and killed his would-be son-in-law's brother – a boy of just ten. And as the father held the bloodstained body of his youngest son in his arms, Karić came up and spat on him.

'If you'd've killed that rotter when you should've, this good'un would still be alive,' Karić said, and with tears in his eyes he fell to his knees before the dead boy. He wept convulsively, kissed the boy's hand and repeated the sad refrain over and over like a scratched record: *Forgive me, forgive me, forgive me...*

'This is all because of you. It's all your fault,' Karić flung at the father as he was being handcuffed and bundled into a police car.

At that moment I realised all the things I miss, all the fascinating stories I don't get to hear, because I refuse to mix with people on principle. People said the son had already been taken to Montenegro's largest jail in Spuž. The inspector who questioned him now sits in his office for hours, drinking, and doesn't speak a word to anyone, they say. But word had already leaked out to willing listeners in the pub next to the police station about what the son said at his questioning, and now the whole town knows the story: *I killed him because he forgave me.*

When he heard that his brother had been killed because of his sin, the son decided to go home for the punishment he felt he had long since deserved. 'I loved my brother more than myself,' people claimed he said. 'As much as I've hated myself all my life, I truly loved my brother,' he allegedly uttered, not caring about the obvious contradictoriness of the statement. In any case, the son returned and stood in front of his father. 'Kill me now at last,' he said. But his father embraced him and burst into tears. 'My son, now you're all I have left. Promise me, swear to me by the grave of your brother, that you'll never leave me again,' his father beseeched him.

The police counted twelve stab wounds on the father's body when they responded to the son's call and the words *I've killed my father.* He waited for them in the hall, still holding the bloodstained kitchen knife in his hand. When he was questioned he admitted everything. 'I have just one condition,' he said. 'I want the death penalty.'

He told them that he'd only come back to Ulcinj to be punished. He returned because he believed his father would kill him for all the evil he'd caused. Taking his own life would have been an option if he'd had the courage, but he admitted he had always been a coward. So he came for the punishment he desperately wanted. Instead, he received forgiveness and couldn't stand it anymore. That's why he killed his father – because he hoped the law would be merciless and someone would finally kill him in return. He admitted everything but demanded the death penalty. 'All my life I've just wanted punishment,' he said. 'I committed every new crime in retaliation for not being punished for the previous one. My father forgave me for everything and that made my life hell,' the son cried before the bewildered police officers. 'You don't know how hard it is to live without punishment, how terrible the world is when there's nothing but forgiveness on the horizon.' After all I'd heard, I found I had the deepest sympathy for him.

Reflecting on how our parents constantly grind us down and destroy us whatever they do, *through their very existence,* just as we grind them down and destroy them through our very existence, I went into one of Ulcinj's myriad cafés and ordered a double whisky at the bar. But I didn't get to drink it in peace because Dirty Djuro came up to me and offered me sex with one of his daughters: 'Just 15 euros for a blow job, just 25 for the real thing.'

Interpersonal relations are a nightmare from which there's no waking up, I thought to myself.

Djuro came to town as a refugee back when the war in Croatia began. He claimed he could repair various appliances and even offered to do it on the cheap. People are miserly and therefore they chose to believe him. It took a few years for them to realise that Djuro never repaired anything for anyone. He'd arrive at a house like an ill omen, called by a householder determined to save money. If Djuro was supposed to fix the fridge, he would remove the motor, and then also offer to 'repair' perfectly functional water heaters, irons and vacuum cleaners. He took a piece out of every appliance and promised to come back the next day with new parts, insert them and reassemble everything he'd dismantled. After he left a house, nothing in it worked anymore. And he did all this damage for just half the price of what tradesmen charged for repairing a single fridge.

As a consequence, not one day went past when he didn't get a beating. Around town, he'd run into the miserly numskulls whose houses he'd devastated and whose appliances remained unfixed because in the meantime he'd sold the parts he removed. The fellow would beat the living daylights out of Djuro, and no sooner had he got to his feet and brushed the dust off, he'd fall to the ground again, bloodied by the blows of one of the local repairmen furious at having their prices undercut and their customers taken away. In the end there was no more work for Djuro, but by then his daughters had grown up and he realised he could earn money on their budding, increasingly curvaceous bodies.

They called him Dirty because his clothes were always slimy like the cassocks of Orthodox priests. And because he pimped his daughters. But whatever people thought of him, they had to admit he was endowed with entrepreneurial spirit. He started business with two of his daughters. The elder, sixteen-year-old Tanja, he advertised as a *buxom blonde who swallows*. The younger, Zorana, who had her first john on her fourteenth birthday, was sold as a *tight, small-breasted brunette*. Later, his third daughter, Mirjana, came of working age and ran as a *sweet anal fantasy*.

Djuro stuck to his low-price policy in prostitution

too. He drove a rusted red Moskvich with *Dirty Djuro &*
Daughters: Sex for Every Pocket painted on the side. Half
an hour later we drove up to his flat in this rattletrap,
looking like something out of a bad film. The old
pervert had detected straight away that I was easy prey.
'Talk about horny – two more whiskys and you'd even
do me! Luckily there are beauties like my daughters,' he
told me.

They lived in a cellar converted into a two-room flat. A
narrow corridor led from there to the business premises
– a three-room brothel. The door was opened for us by
Djuro's wife, a gap-toothed old lady with breasts worn
out from feeding the horde of children who gambolled
about the flat like a litter of puppies. Her face spoke of
a great weariness and the desire for an early death. I was
wondering what was left for a mother of three, four
or five children, when suddenly two more appeared,
making a total of seven. When someone multiplies life
to such an extent, even if they don't understand it, they
at least feel its worthlessness. Children are like money:
the more of it you print, the more of them you bear, the
less they're worth.

This hyperinflation of children hampered our
forward progress through Djuro's flat. As soon as the
children saw me, they ran towards me. The burliest of
them, and thus the most dangerous, grabbed me by my
trousers with chocolate-smeared hands. Another knelt
in front of me and cried, announcing a demand I didn't
understand and which obviously had nothing to do with
me anyway. A third, the smallest one, bit into my shoe.

51

'Don't worry, he's just teething,' Djuro told me. 'Follow me, I'll take you to Tanja.'

I carefully shook off the ankle-biter, not wanting to break his milk teeth, and headed after Djuro.

'Look, I've made sure that each has her own room,' he said. He wanted me to know that he was a devoted father. They were young women now and needed to have intimacy. Besides, he added, there was no need to economise on space because he'd made a good deal with the tenants. In return for being able to use the whole cellar, the family offered them sex for free.

'They're all old men and don't want it more than once a month,' he confided in me. 'And imagine: there are some who want my wife. You can give them beauties like my daughters, but the old farts want my wife – that old walrus!' he sniggered.

We went into Tanja's room. She was lying on the bed in black underwear. I noticed that her knickers were frayed at the edges. She pursed her fleshy, shoddily made-up lips in an effort to look sensual. The bra holding her enormous breasts was smeared with sperm. I handed Djuro the money and pushed him out of the room.

'I've had my eye on you for a while,' Tanja said. 'But I didn't make any advances because I thought: a cool cat like him can have any woman he wants, so why would he pay for me?'

'Very flattering of you,' I mumbled and tried to have a look around the room. But she hadn't finished.

'You'd be surprised if you knew how many well-to-do, handsome men come to see me.'

'Believe me, I'm not surprised,' I told her.

'But it's clever ones like you who turn me on the most,' she purred, looking me in the eyes.

We find a bent for the intellectual in the most unexpected of places, I thought. Everyone is driven by the eternal *Why*: the physicist in a Zürich laboratory, the art historian in the Vatican Library and the whore in Ulcinj. They're all equally far from, and thus equally close to, an answer: it's just as appropriate and legitimate to seek answers in atoms, books or smelly provincial phalluses. Therefore, everyone has equal right to intellectual snobbery – or rather no right – and everyone pondering the questions of existence is equally laughable.

I was blessed by an interruption in the conversation because Tanja now devoted herself to her ritual of cleansing. Leaning over the washstand, she soaped up the coves of her armpits and then the fjord between her legs. She hummed a cheerful melody; I think it was *Put on something folky, let's do the pokey-pokey*. Finally, I had time to study her room.

On the camp bed, leaning against the metal bars, was a teddy bear. It faced a pink pillow in the shape of a heart. Beneath the bed I saw an open book; something by Virginia Woolf. Probably *A Room of One's Own*. Tanja tried to satisfy as broad a target group as possible, I said to myself. The camp bed was for the sadists, the teddy bear and the pink pillow were to please the paedophiles, and the book was for intellectuals like me but could also come in handy for slapping the masochists. Djuro's family left nothing to coincidence – it was a well-organised, carefully thought-out, proper little family business.

That's what I thought until I saw the photo on the wall above Tanja's bed. It was of her and her father, embracing and smiling. They were standing on the terrace above *Mala Plaža* beach with the open sea behind them on a fine spring day: the air was clean and radiant, and the world was steeped in a blue we otherwise see only in toilet-cleaner ads. Djuro hugged his daughter around the neck, laughing and kissing her hair. One of her arms hung around his waist. She was looking up at her father, and he was leaning down towards her. Her eyes were full of adoration and love in just the way that young women in the paintings of the Old Masters look up into the sky, searching for God, or at least the saints. She really must love her father, I thought. Ten minutes beforehand she'd had sex with a man who her father pimped her to. And it wasn't hard to imagine that he'd take her off for another fat toad of a man to lie on, straight after the photo was taken. Her father had made a whore of her and ruined any chance of her ever being anything else, at least in a small town like this where everyone knows everything and nothing is ever forgotten. She was forever doomed to be a cheap whore, thanks to her father. For as long as she lived she would put out to old men and pimply teenagers because that was the only future she had: ever-worse customers and ever-lower prices. And then death in contempt and loneliness, if she didn't get AIDS first or some maniac cut her throat or suffocated her with a pillow. All that because of her father. Yet despite all that, she looked up at him with a love which couldn't be faked.

I left the room in a hurry. Traversing the kitchen in the greatest urgency, I was waylaid by Djuro.

'Let me introduce you: this is my mysterious son Petar. "Why mysterious?" you may ask yourself,' he blathered, although I was only asking myself how to flee that cellar as quickly as possible.

I breathed with difficulty because I suddenly became aware of the claustrophobic quality of the space around me, and that feeling merged with a growing rage inside me.

'He's mysterious because no-one knows who his father is,' Dirty Djuro guffawed. 'Look at him: a donkey of sixteen, a handsome lad, but he doesn't look like his father – his *alleged* father, I should say,' Djuro snarled and spat.

Then he grabbed the lad by the ears.

'As to who his father is, you'll have to ask my wife. I only know he's not mine. Either my wife is a whore or he was sent by God to test me, like Father Bogdan said. I don't believe in God, but I fear Him. So I say to myself: in case this is some kind of test, I'd better tolerate the little guy till he grows up. One more mouth to feed? I won't even notice. But just look at him –,' he shouted and grabbed the lad by the genitals, 'talk about well hung, eh? Anyway, I've done my part of the deal with God: if this is His child, then I've been good to him like a real father...'

I heard the tail-end of Djuro's theological dilemma as I fled from the cellar where that big happy family lived in harmony and love. I hurried to make it back to my car because I couldn't spend a second longer amid the river of flesh pouring towards the promenade and the cafés. These were anthills emitting *turbofolk* music and the beastly odour of humans ready to copulate. And so I desperately strove against the current of the Styx, which was dragging me back into that seething human crowd. I felt I was sinking in a human multitude like a person going under. Drowning in humanity – what a terrible way to go!

Somehow I made it to the pavement and leaned, panting, against a pole to catch my breath, finally out of harm's way. 'Hey mate!' I heard and flinched. 'My old friend!' the voice went on, and now a heavy hand was laid on my shoulder. I stared at those fingers with skin as rough as the bark of a centennial tree and as thick and knotted as Montenegrin mountain sausages. Each of those fingers seemed strong enough to squash the life out of me, but I wasn't afraid of them at all, nor was I afraid of the wielder of such powerful and at the same time absurd fingers. Everything is equally absurd, even that which kills us. We realise that as soon as we overcome our fear of what threatens to destroy us. I laughed, gazing at the grime under the giant fingernails. I was amused by the thought that anyone could kill me, even a man who doesn't use nail clippers – someone so primitive that he doesn't even clean under his nails.

'It's you, mate!' yelled the giant, who was now standing

in front of me. I measured him from head to foot. What I saw was a six-foot-something, 300-pound hulk, his shaggy hair encrusted with cement – *so he's a building worker*, I thought, and with bloodshot eyes in a yellow face – *so he's an alcoholic with a destroyed liver*. His cheap, tattered jeans and worn-out army boots, in which he seemed to step-dance in front of me, only confirmed the sad sketch I'd made out at first glance.

The colossus evidently knew me. As if that wasn't compromising enough for me already, he expected me to recognise him. 'It's me, Uroš!' he shouted, making all the passers-by turn and look at us, like we were game-show contestants and they were the crowd, allowed to be malicious spectators of my humiliation.

Uroš was an unlucky wretch I went to school with until Year 8. After years of daily abuse, the gang of kids set on him by arch-bully Žarko Primorac broke both his arms. Uroš's dim-witted parents were determined for their son to have the education they didn't, but this event finally made them decide to take him out of school, and by all indications he didn't re-enrol. Uroš was my best, or, if you like, my only school friend. The day they broke his arms I was standing in the corner of the schoolyard like I did every day. I munched away at my hamburger and watched the ever-bloodthirsty onlookers form a circle around Primorac's bully boys and Uroš, whom they spat on and kicked every day. I never said a word in his defence, and obviously I never ran up to offer help. I'd just eat my lunch and wait until the mob had had enough of inflicting torment and humiliation and split up. Uroš would wipe the blood from his face and come over to sit next to me. He never blamed me or expected me to do anything for him.

Now he did. He expected, even insisted, that we go and sit in a nearby café and have a drink. When people grow up they lose the few good traits they had as kids, I thought. That's why we're always disappointed when we meet long-lost childhood friends. Friendship is ultimately only possible in childhood because the concept of it demands a naivety which only childhood can ensure. Only children and idiots can have *friends*. That's a word that goes together with an exuberant *ta-da-da-da!* Who else, other than children and idiots (i.e. the larger part of humanity) could believe there exist people so noble and good that we could believe them, confide our innermost thoughts and feelings in them and expect their help when things take a turn for the worse, which in all honesty things always do. If someone manages to cultivate what they consider *a lifelong friendship*, that merely means the friendship hasn't been properly put to the test. There's no friendship which won't crumble beneath the weight of a friend's bad character or the weight of evil, which all people are condemned to carry in their very core due to the very nature of being human.

'So how are you doing, my old friend?' Uroš yelled.

Seeing as he'd interrupted me in contemplation, he deserved for me to be ruthless, so I replied, 'Sorry, but I was just thinking about something. Be quiet for ten minutes, remember what you wanted to say and tell me later.' And good old Uroš really did fall silent.

He guzzled his beer and grinned, evidently managing to convince himself that he was glad to see me. When people resolve to be good-hearted you can do what you want with them – it's simply impossible to offend them. And that's fair enough. To be good-hearted means to transcend oneself and to rise above one's own nature, therefore so-called 'good people' use their 'goodness' to create an unforgettable pleasure for themselves, one of the most profound a person can feel. They enjoy their own goodness to such an extent that the rest of us have no obligations towards them whatsoever. In fact, the worse we behave towards them, the greater is their goodness towards us, and thus the pleasure they're rewarded with is also greater.

'Well then, Uroš, how's life treating you?' I said when I'd finally resolved to speak to him.

'Pretty well,' he replied. 'Can't complain.'

In the first few years after his parents had taken him out of school he refused to leave the farm and go into town, he told me.

'You know, I was really offended by what Primorac and his guys did to me,' he said almost apologetically, as if he was telling me amazing things I'd find hard to believe. 'I felt kind of humiliated. Things were fine on the farm. But in town I might run into one of my old school friends.' Those were his words, *school friends*. 'I forgave them, but I never wanted to see them again. That's why I avoided town.'

Then the war broke out. His father told him to enlist in the army to go and fight in Bosnia.

'And that's what I did,' he said, and I believed him.

That's just like him, I thought – he never used to ask any questions.

'I killed a few people in the war. Later it gave me sleepless nights, but over time you get used to things,' he explained, and went on to present his pitiable philosophy of life. 'I always forgive myself. Whatever you do, you always accept yourself again afterwards, isn't that right? Each of us does terrible things which we're mortally ashamed of, but we keep on living. That's why I wasn't angry at the guys who bashed me up back at school – I knew all the bad things I'd done, and if I forgive myself it's only fair that I forgive them. To think badly of others you have to think well of yourself, and I can't do that. I know myself pretty well and I know I'm no better than others.'

He killed during the war, but he stayed in the background whenever he was ordered to burn houses and rape women, he told me.

'I hid then, I must admit, but I'm no coward. When there was shooting, I fired like the others. But I couldn't do anything to the women. I felt sorry for them and simply couldn't do it with them. Others did, but not me. Maybe it was because I myself was maltreated as a boy. Could that have been it?' he asked me.

He returned home. The next winter his parents married him off, and he and his wife came to live in town.

'In Ulcinj we had it better than in the country. Now that I had a wife I was sort of proud and didn't care

60

what others thought of me,' he said.

Sometimes he'd run into those who'd abused him. Some of them looked at him with a derisive smile, others with shame. One of those he met was Žarko Primorac.

'He came up to me, and God was he friendly! He invited me for a few drinks. After we'd had two or three he started apologising,' Uroš told me. 'We were at the bar for a long time that evening. And he cried, man did he cry! In the end I took him home to my place, and all the way he held my hand. He gripped it like a vice, as if he was hanging over an abyss and my hand was the last thing for him to cling to. And he didn't let go of it until I promised we'd see each other again.

'When my son was born, Primorac became the godfather. He was always considerate of my Miloš. He never forgot a single birthday, Easter or Christmas, and would always come with presents,' Uroš said. 'To tell the truth, I'd never have been able to buy him things like that, so let his godfather, I thought. If I, his father, work on a building site from dawn till dusk just to make ends meet, let him have toys from Primorac if that's the only way he can have them. The boy's got it hard enough because of my poverty, and it's not his fault.

'Then I had a chance to go and work in Nigeria for six months,' he said, as if it had been a lucky break. 'I slaved my guts out like here, but at least the money was better. When I came back I took a taxi home. The whole boot was crammed full of presents – both for her and for Miloš. *Now I'm going to give them something nice for a change,* I thought. *All the presents from Primorac have made my son like him more than he likes his own father.*

'Nena, the old landlady, was waiting in the courtyard. She burst into tears when she saw me,' Uroš said. 'I asked her what was wrong and where my family was, but she didn't answer. She just cried and said *My good Uroš* over and over again. *Where's my wife?* I asked her. I wanted to go into the house, but Nena stood in front of me and wouldn't let me in. *You no longer have a family or a home, my good Uroš,* she told me.

'So, old mate, my wife had left me. And who with? With Primorac the godfather, of course, and she took our son with her. They didn't even wait a week after I'd gone, Nena told me. They got up early one morning, packed their things before dawn so the neighbours wouldn't see, hopped in the van and were gone. They didn't call anyone, so no-one knows where they went. I looked for them for a while but then gave up. I drank my Nigerian pay – it had only brought me bad luck anyway. *And may it be the death of you,* I said to myself. I didn't leave the bar until I'd drunk away the very last dollar. There's no way, mate – if you live all your life with nothing, you'll end up with nothing. And if I had anything but straw in my head, I would've known that money isn't for me. I had everything except for money. Then I went after money and lost everything,' he said.

He didn't blame anyone except himself, he added, and he forgave both his wife and Primorac. He only missed his son. But he hoped that Miloš would come and look for him one day. He hoped he'd remember his old dad when he grew up and, wherever he was now, that he'd return to Ulcinj to see him, if only for a day. Yet Uroš still knew that nothing mattered and it was *all the same* – a phrase which had become the refrain of his life.

'You know, I've thought a lot about everything. I've had the time,' he said laughing. 'I mean, what else are you going to do when you're left all alone? I thought a lot, and in the end I realised *it's all the same*. And if I hadn't run into Žarko Primorac in the street that day, and if he hadn't shouted me drinks, and if we'd drunk by the glass and not by the bottle, and if I hadn't felt sorry for him when he cried, and if I hadn't promised we'd see each other again, and if I hadn't taken him home to my place, where he met my wife – it still would have been *all the same*, because everything would've been up shit creek anyway.

'Even if Žarko Primorac had had one ounce of decency in him, which he didn't, and if he'd remembered that he'd already done me ill enough for the rest of my life – after all, they carried me out of school with broken arms, and because of him I never went back – and if he'd remembered that that sentenced me to mix cement and cast concrete for the rest of my life, and if he'd realised that it was he who destroyed any chance of me ever being more than a day labourer, which he didn't, and if that had made him think *I'll never do him harm again*, which it didn't, and if everything had turned out differently, it would still be *all the same*.

'The Devil would've found a way of fleecing me, I realised in the end, because I've never had any luck, and never will have,' he said. 'Whatever I do, it'll be *all the same* – I'll croak it alone, and the last thing that'll pass through my head will be: *Die properly now, and may all the misfortune die with you!*

'Miloš can come and see me, and maybe his biggest wish when he grows up will be to see his father. But what will he see? A shabby, dirty drunkard with a scraggly beard who sleeps in derelict workers' huts, washes once a month, eats every second day and is dying of a bleeding liver because he's had his fill of every kind of poison in this life: from what you drink in the bar because you want to and what you down every day because you have to – because others say you must. What should Miloš do? If he comes and sees me like this, I'll die of shame that my son has seen how wretched I am. And if he doesn't come, I'll die of shame that not even my own son cares about me. Whatever's in store, it's *all the same* to me. Just like it's *all the same* to him, too. If he comes, he'll be haunted by shame until his dying day because of what his father was like. If he doesn't come, regret will catch up with him: he'll remember the day that his father died and he didn't go to see him, and he'll feel ashamed because of it. Whatever he does, he'll be dogged by misfortune, just like everything I ever did was plagued by misfortune. And so you see, my friend, that's why nothing matters to me.'

I thought for a moment that I should pay for our drinks because I'm rich, after all, and he's poor. But I let him pay because it was *all the same*, just like he said. We should never prevent people from putting their money where their mouth is. Although he had to turn his pockets inside out to find enough money to pay with, he was in good spirits when he left.

'I'm glad to have met you again,' he said, and was gone before I could answer.

Actually, I'd really wanted to tell him an edifying and comforting story, something about the Austrian writer Thomas Bernhard. It always soothes me to think of Bernhard because we cannot but feel comfort when we hear of others' misfortune being greater than our own. If I'd managed to tell Uroš about Bernhard, he would have gone to sleep happy that night. Because I would have told him that the story teaches us an important thing: that human misfortune is always the same and equally possible everywhere. A starving farmer in the paddy fields of Asia and a depressive writer languidly chewing *Sachertorte* and sipping *Julius Meinl* coffee in a Viennese café have equal reason to be unhappy. We have equally good reason to be unhappy, he and I, because human misfortune doesn't derive from a social system or a geographical location, but from existence itself. Simply *to be somewhere* is reason enough to be unhappy. Actually, it's enough just *to be*. I'd tell him that others have also been *cast into life,* just like we have, and condemned to an existence we didn't want, just like us. It was like that both for him, who had to walk to school from his village in worn-out shoes, and for me, who was driven to school by his father every morning in the Mercedes bought with his uncle's money. Both for him, who went hungry all through school, and for me, who knew that but never offered to buy him a stupid school lunch. Both for him and for Žarko Primorac, who paid the ever-hungry and venal proletarian children with doughnuts and pastries so they'd abuse Uroš in the schoolyard, and do it during the break so that his humiliation was public and visible to all, and thus all the more terrible for him. Both for him and Žarko Primorac, and for me, who never ran up to offer help. And for the suckers who'd bolt down the food Primorac bought them, wipe their mouths on their sleeves and get down to the job. They bashed Uroš mercilessly although they had nothing against him. But they beat him diligently to make sure their boss was satisfied and would buy them delicacies the next day, too. If Primorac hadn't found Uroš particularly repugnant and if it hadn't been for his sadistic urge to abuse and humiliate him, they'd never have eaten chocolate-filled doughnuts in their impoverished early years. Uroš did suffer, but they got the doughnuts they'd craved for every day of their hungry childhoods. Yep, that's probably what they think of when people say *every cloud has a silver lining*. He and I do, too, to the same degree. If he'd just let me tell him that, he'd have been able to realise how comforting it is.

But Uroš undoubtedly saw I was unhappy. He had to see it because the first thing people think when they meet me is: *God, how unhappy that man is*. That's why he said 'I'm glad to have met you again'. He probably said the same thing to Primorac when he went boozing with him, I thought, because it was clear that Primorac was unhappy too. How great is the joy of those who envied us our apparent childhood *happiness* when they meet us as adults and see that life has made us just as unhappy as them. Life levels us all in misfortune and despair, and every advantage we once had turns against us. But it drives those deprived of all chances, like Uroš, beyond rage and bitterness, and they end up in shame. Instead of being resentful towards others and towards life itself, he awaits the end in shame. Ultimately, Uroš, who was abused by Primorac, could find consolation solely in the fact that life maltreated Primorac too. Each of us is both an executioner and a victim – everyone abuses everyone else. The sadist will come to feel like a martyr sooner or later, and a martyr who lives long enough will also commit contemptible acts which will ensure lasting notoriety. There was nothing else for tormented Primorac to do but to enjoy the feeling of once having been the one who abused: he remembered that when he encountered Uroš. That's why he was so glad to have met him again. That meeting of executioner and victim was to their mutual satisfaction, which is a real rarity in the rich and complex history of executioner and victim, so fraught with negative emotions.

I thought about Uroš as I cruised through town in my car. The rough road took me up to the TV transmitter on Pinješ Hill. I stopped the car and sat there, sipping my whisky and looking at the lights of the town. I located the CD I'd burned for moments of particular desperation. It had two tracks on it – *John Walker's Blues* by Steve Earle and *Leif Erikson* by Interpol – and I played them over and over until I'd emptied the bottle.

That's why I dipped into humanity again: to buy more blasted whisky. That was the only reason for socialising that night. I bought two flasks of Glenfiddich, sat in front of the supermarket and downed several fiery gulps. The golden fluid would flow and I'd find the strength to move back to the car.

But it seemed that not even such a simple plan could be achieved. However little we expect of life, it gives us even less. Disappointment is inevitable, and not even the complete absence of hope can free us of it. I only wanted to drink whisky and then run away home. Instead, I was forced into a conversation with Samir the Wahabi.

I could see him striding towards me like a harbinger of doom. He came straight at me, and the people he bumped into on the way were flung back as if they'd hit a brick wall. If there could be an Islamic comic superhero, some kind of Arabian Hulk, it would look like him, I remember thinking. Even while he was still some way off, I saw he was yelling at me and waving his index finger threateningly.

Samir was usually harmless. You would find him standing around town with his thick black beard and funny white crocheted cap. He was a bogeyman for infidels on his gnarled legs, whose lankiness was further emphasised by the baggy, three-quarter pants he wore. Ranting and raving, he warned the people of Ulcinj about sin and doom. He was therefore considered a local loony, one of many.

Samir had once been a promising young talent, a

brilliant pianist, whose rendition of Bach's *Goldberg Variations* had brought him to the cusp of fame. He was invited to study piano at the Mozarteum University in Salzburg, which he accepted, and the people of Ulcinj saw him as a 'local boy made good' who had a great future ahead of him, predicting that he was sure to become one of the world's leading pianists. But just two years later he came back. Some said he'd been raped: that a group of students had abused him on the piano and then whipped him with conductor's batons as he staggered, bleeding from the anus, all the way from the recital hall back to the dorm. Others spoke of an Austrian girl he'd been due to marry. They loved each other and were happy, until one evening she was found hanging from an oak tree in front of the Mozarteum. According to that story, she wrote in a farewell letter that she'd chosen to die because her parents wouldn't allow her to marry him, and she wouldn't marry any other. Apparently, the letter was sewed to her belly with red thread and stated *I'm leaving, my love, and taking our unborn child with me*, but the abundance of details made that version seem less convincing.

Whatever really happened, Samir sought consolation in the mosque. The fingers which had once flown over the piano keys now turned the pages of the Koran. What Austria hadn't given him, he now received from Saudi Arabia. People could scoff at Samir while he stood at the traffic lights berating and Koran-bashing them, and they also felt pity for him. But I envied him, because the only truly happy person is the zealot prepared to put everything on the line for what they believe. Of course, what we believe reveals itself as a lie in the end, and what we were prepared to give everything for turns out not to have been worth a thing, not even something as trifling as our life. But that disappointment comes later. Before it grips us, before reason sets in and the tide demolishes the sandcastle we've placed all our hopes in, the moments of happiness we live are the only ones we will have. I never had that hope, and that's why I envied Samir. One moment of blind faith in anything, even in the most utter nonsense, brings a person more happiness than all the reason and knowledge in the world; for reason and knowledge do nothing but destroy any possibility of happiness and reveal everything we've tried to link our life to as worthless. That's why we float like balloons, bloated to bursting point with reason, just waiting for the moment when one tiny extra bit of knowledge will blow us to smithereens – when our body, as fragile as the membrane of a balloon, explodes from the despair which fills us.

When he stood in front of me and sent me what must have been his best reproachful look, I finally understood what he was saying to me.

'You'd better put away that bottle!' he commanded. 'Don't bring more evil upon yourself. I can see there's more than enough of it in you already. Don't you know it's forbidden to consume alcohol?'

'Of course, but not for me – I'm not a Muslim,' I said.

'I know *very well* who you are,' Samir replied. (Why not come out and say he knows *everything* about me?

I thought.) 'I know that your great-grandfather was an Orthodox priest, and that's why I'm appealing to you — because the Bible also forbids alcohol.'

I tried to explain to him that I'm a non-Christian to the same extent that I'm a non-Muslim, as well as telling him that all I knew about my great-grandfather was that he was an idiot who plunged his family into misery with his religion. Nothing that Samir had to say from now until eternity was of any interest to me, so I asked him politely to go away and leave me in peace. He replied that he saw evil in me, that even among the throng in town that night he could see evil radiating from me.

Then all at once he changed his tone. He calmed down, pulled up one of the Coca-Cola crates and sat next to me.

'I'm whispering because they're everywhere around us. I can see them following you like they follow me,' he said.

We sat on crates there in front of the supermarket: one of us drunk on alcohol and the other with religion, but both with a vision of evil and ruin around him. Samir told me he believed we were both being pursued by spirits. He claimed they were called djinns.

He spoke eloquently and what he said was not uninteresting, but it certainly was threatening. As we know, the only things we take seriously are those which threaten us.

'Allah, blessed be His name, said: *We made the djinns of scorching fire.* According to some it was the fire of lightning, others say it was the fire of the sun,' Samir explained.

Then he demanded that I reject the image of the world I have.

'There is no one single reality. Reality is tiered and consists of three worlds: material, psychic and spiritual,' he declared mechanically. 'The djinns live between this world, where you and I are now, and the world of pure spirit – they're denizens of the psychic world,' he said, tapping his finger against his forehead.

'The djinns have no permanent shape and can therefore take any form. They have a soul and therefore, like man, are responsible to Allah. Some of the djinns are on the right path and are Muslims. Others are forces of evil in the struggle against Allah. They lurk in the shadows waiting for us and are constantly assailing us,' he told me, visibly agitated. 'They attack me when I'm praying, just like they attack you when you're drinking. But I defend myself again and again, while you give in to them.

'Sometimes you can hear them at night and it sounds like they're romping around your bed. Sometimes they look like ghosts, other times like dogs. Beware of the black dogs in particular! The Prophet said: *The black dog is a Devil! Were dogs not a species of creature, I should command that they all be killed. But I am afraid to kill a whole species. Even so: kill all black dogs because they are djinns.* Those were the words of the Prophet,' Samir claimed.

I learnt from him that evening that being unclean, both physically and spiritually, opened the door to the djinns. When I masturbated I flung the door wide open to evil, he warned me, and I realised that it would be hard for me to ever close it again! According to Samir, masturbation was a call to evil to take us over. When it did, there was only one way to expel it: by turning to what is holy. He explained that the djinns flee from the holy, just as they flee from light and water.

'What is dark must be made light, and what is impure must be cleansed.' With that he abruptly got up and, without looking back, vanished among the crowd of people who were unaware of the danger awaiting them and lived their lives open for evil.

My good Samir, I thought as I lurched off towards the car: everyone is evil and everyone is a liar. As long as you search for evil around you, you're blind to the evil within, and everything is inside you.

That's how my father used to speak to me. He'd sit in his armchair on the terrace for hours, as if petrified, and read Saint Augustine's *Confessions*. If he hadn't moved his hand from time to time, just to turn the page, you really would have thought he'd turned to stone. He sought refuge in that immobility, erecting barricades against everything around him, and whenever he said anything it felt like a stony monument was addressing me. He only spoke words of warning and censure because his self-seclusion and hermit-like asceticism evidently gave him the strength to judge me. This was only possible because he'd never been strong enough to pass judgement on himself – he'd always been weak and indecisive. In the end, he fled beneath the skirts of Saint Augustine, read him, and assumed the pose of a statue of him. Surely he can't have thought that would be sufficient for his salvation; surely he can't have seen a salutary *transcendental* and a *vertical* in it, to use his words.

'You can't run and hide – all your holy-roller stuff is in vain because none of it is real,' I yelled at him. 'There's only torment, for which you're too weak. Some flee from it into death and decay, and some into religion, which also ultimately leads to death and decay. There's only the torment, from which you all flee; and there's me, determined to endure every little bit of the agony I've been granted for as long as I exist,' I shouted.

He pointed a trembling finger at me and muttered his Augustine: *You are one of those who live their life ever destroying and never creating; all that is good comes from God, and all evil from human freedom to choose.*

That was our last quarrel. I left him on the terrace with Bach playing on the gramophone and Augustine in his hands, all alone in that empty house which he filled with the transcendental after my mother died. We told each other all we had to say and then I left him for good. Since then, we've known nothing about each other, just as we knew nothing of each other before. We've felt nothing but antipathy for each other and yet we regretted that things had to be this way. Regretted that we never really had a chance for love to grow between us.

The fastest and least unpleasant way back to the car led through the abandoned underground car park. From there I knew I'd be able to squeeze my way through the row of ramshackle houses to the park, and then walk up the alleyways to Pinješ Hill, where I'd parked the car. The risk of running into someone I didn't want to meet, if we abstract from the fact that I never want to meet anyone, was minimal. This shortcut to the car led round the back of the multitude thronging in their own sweat and stench on the promenade in search of summer amusements. It led through the dark beyond the reach of the street lights, under which tens of thousands of people bobbed and collided in their mindless trajectories like a disarrayed army of ants trundling the same streets as they did every evening, every summer.

Near the deserted Socialist-era supermarket, there was a car park from which a broad staircase led underground. The Communist leaders, recruited from the impoverished proletariat and simple-minded peasantry, made up for their modest origins by hatching megalomaniac plans for the future. They saw everything they built as their own tombstone – that which future generations would remember them by, because they believed in the idiotic idea that human life doesn't end at death but endures through people's deeds.

Once I read in the local paper that the car park with its three levels covered every bit of 100,000 square feet. This was not including the nuclear shelter, whose dimensions are unknown since the information is still treated as a military secret. The building would make a perfect vault or crypt, and I assume it would be possible to transfer the remains of all the Yugoslav Communist leaders there. In the process, the coffins of their immediate family members could also be brought to the shelter so that they could be together in death, too. The Yugoslav Marxists lived according to the maxim that the family is the basic building block of society, so it seemed appropriate that the same social organisation should be upheld in the afterlife, too.

But this gargantuan child was useless as a car park. When the weary tradesmen had completed the final construction tasks and the pig-faced municipal president cut the ribbon to declare the place open, no car could drive into it accompanied by the town sirens' festive blare. The underground car park was ready but lacked a short stretch of access road. The newspapers of the time justified a car park which no cars could enter as being 'part of the anticipated dynamic development of the town'. The car park was just the first step: the next five-year plan would see 'construction of the road into and out of the car park, as well as a range of associated infrastructural facilities to enhance the attractiveness of the Ulcinj area as a tourist destination'. The municipal president delivered his vision of the future road in a speech to a meeting of the town's youth. The gist of his argument went like this: if today's generations went and built *everything*, meaning the car park *and* the access road, they'd run the risk of pampering generations to come. Just as their fathers had done a hard job by fighting for and winning the country's freedom, they too had done a hard job by building the car park. Every new generation had it easier: half a century ago we had nothing; now we had our freedom and the car park; the access road was the only thing missing. These were his main points, and it revealed a glimpse of the future concept of development. The car park was evidently conceived as a story without end – an everlasting building site which every generation would contribute to until the end of the world.

In the meantime, however, the car park was a hole in the centre of town, where the local population disposed of their rubbish on a daily basis. And as I was going down the stairs into this notorious rubbish dump, I almost tripped over rusty television sets and fridges several times, along with piles of good old jumbo rubbish bags which the more environmentally conscious citizens dispose their refuse in. The light bulbs which had not yet been smashed by the local hooligans flickered in an effort to illuminate this mausoleum to the belief in progress.

The abandoned car park provided the inspiration for many local urban legends. It began with the story about a band of drug addicts who gathered *under the town*. Then a dead girl was found in the car park. She'd been raped, some said. Others claimed the killer had cut off both her hands before she died. The police ultimately reported that the girl had died from tumbling down the stairs, and that she'd tumbled down the stairs because she wanted to, and that she'd wanted to because she was the victim of a paedophile, incestuous father, which caused her to commit suicide and saw her father end up in jail. But before it irrefutably became a 'family tragedy', the case ran the gauntlet of neighbourhood gossip, with every teller of the story inserting some figment of their darkest desires and frustrations. They said the girl had been anally gang-raped. Or that she'd been forced to have oral sex, again with several men. Or that she was found with her eyes gouged out, which meant that suspicions were directed towards the Satanists. Or that her kidneys had been plucked out, which saw the blame being levelled at the human-organ traffickers who'd passed themselves off as an old married couple from Italy and managed to deceive their victims with the image of friendly, senile tourists travelling the impoverished European fringe to bring humanitarian aid to the local population. The dead girl was a blank slate, and the town testified to its own repulsiveness. Let people give free rein to their fantasies and hell will open up before you. A smelly sulphurous torrent of their thoughts will gush forth, full of slimy desires spawned from their souls like monstrously deformed infants; full of suppressed fears dredged up from that cemetery of bones and putrid corpses inside.

There were a few more fantasy murders as well as several real suicides down in the car park, which became a chasm into which the people of Ulcinj stuck everything they didn't dare to say or even think, like in the fable about the emperor who had goat's ears but banned anyone from saying so. But no hole is deep enough to accommodate all the evil of humanity. If someone managed to wring all the black out of just one human soul, like the ink from a squid, the whole world would disappear in murk. Only demented minds could split atoms and search with microscopes for the perfect weapon; just peer into one human being and you'll find all that's required to obliterate life on Earth.

When I was down in the car park I felt comfortable for the first time that evening. I'd always known there's no place people can find happiness except underground. Up above me humanity raged, producing a clamour which penetrated even the thick reinforced concrete of the construction. The footsteps above my head sounded like tiny nails being hammered into the coffin I'd voluntarily entered. Alas, even below ground I wasn't alone: one unpleasant surprise follows another – that's the story of my life.

I sat on a heap of abandoned books at the nethermost point of the car park, in front of the giant steel doors of the nuclear shelter, and browsed through some of them. There was quite a collection of religious trash: *One Hundred Ways to Attain Salvation*, *Interpreting God's Signs* and *Self-Awareness*. I lit a cigarette and looked attentively at the piles of rubbish around me. The harsh landscape of garbage is comforting, devoid as it is of promise, and thus of hope and subsequent disappointment. Everything around me was spent, disposed of and utterly forgotten, as if it had never existed. I sympathised with every one of the discarded domestic appliances, kitchen cabinets and light fixtures. Each of us awaits the same fate which befell them. People will use us and then forget us just like they used and forgot those objects. Intermittently, people are useful to us for some reason and so we bond with them. But the very next day, they bother us and we wish for nothing more than for them to vanish from our lives. Every day we discard people like we discard rubbish.

We discard and will be discarded, that's the simple truth. We're cast into a world which constantly discards us. In the end we're left alone with ourselves to wander the waste dump of our lives. All around us are discarded friends, lovers, and people good for one day; those we avoided and those we got rid of.

For a moment, I thought I saw the silhouette of a person between two old fridges. I told myself not to be ridiculous, that no-one had come here for years. The locals think the place is cursed, and tourists only come down for a pee or, in moments of great sexual urgency, to have an unfulfilling quickie. But they never come down this far. Whatever brings them here, they perform it at the base of the stairs, from where they still have a comforting glimpse of the world above them.

Despite the convincing argument I consoled myself with, the silhouette emerged from the darkness again. In front of me now stood a dark-skinned boy. He looked at me with a measured gaze, his eyes full of suspicion. Then he held out his hand to me, which I naturally took as an extremely hostile gesture.

The impertinence of beggars knows no bounds. They're people who demand compassion from us again and again, despite them having none for others. They act as if there was no other misfortune in the universe apart from theirs. When a person dear to you dies and you drive the streets of the town in despair, waiting for the sedatives you've swallowed to take effect, you stop at the traffic lights and a beggar woman with a child pinned like a brooch to her flaccid breast will come up and ask you for money. What does she care for your suffering? She's got enough of her own and is determined to get something in exchange for it. Even in the midst of the worst tragedy that could befall you, beggars will still stubbornly assail you, demanding that you pay them for *their* tragedy. And if a person, in their greatest despair, decided to end their life by jumping off a high-rise building, I'm sure the beggars would reach their hands out through the staircase windows and demand alms from the plummeting figure.

As if that wasn't enough, beggars also unscrupulously exploit their physical deficiencies. Once at the traffic lights near the railway station in Podgorica, a Gypsy stuck his withered leg in through the open window of my car. I hadn't noticed him as he came up, pulling himself along on his crutches. With the cool calmness of a hit man, he thrust his leg in through the window and kicked me in the face; his foot stank abominably. I hastily opened the door, knocking him back and into the adjacent lane, right in front of a truck which had stopped at the red light. With a bit of luck I was able to push the bastard beneath the moving vehicle. He got up onto his crutches again with amazing speed and came at me again, cursing. Fortunately, I had a can of Coca-Cola in the car, the perfect projectile, which I landed right between his evil little eyes. This time he hit the asphalt properly. In my rear-view mirror I saw the blood trickle from his forehead onto the asphalt. Later, when the police questioned me, they asked why I fled the 'scene of the accident', as they called it. I told them that the formulation 'scene of the accident' was quite inappropriate to my mind because the event had really made my day.

'You fled because you didn't have the courage to face up to what you did,' the officer shouted.

I explained to him that I only drove away because the traffic lights had turned green and the impatient drivers behind me were blowing their horns, unwilling to let me revel in what I'd done and savour the sight of that miscreant bowled over backwards.

Now here I was, faced with another such situation; the boy with the outstretched hand edged towards me, step by cautious step. Uh-oh, I thought, a misfortune never comes alone: behind him several more beggars brazenly stepped forth from what I had considered the dark of non-existence. I counted them: there was one man, two women, and five children of indeterminable sex. Now that a whole family of beggars had appeared, I realised I'd better get out of there quickly. One of the women had a lump on her back the size of a mirror ball in your average disco, while the other's face was wrapped in bandages embellished with bloodstains. Both of them were also lacking vital limbs; at least an arm and a leg each, I estimated at first glance. But their anatomic minimalism didn't mean the effacement of all beauty, and I discerned something well-proportioned about their figures, a kind of pragmatic symmetry. One of the women lacked a left arm and a right leg, while the other lacked a right arm and a left leg, so the diagonal presence and diagonal absence of limbs intersected on their bodies. This symmetry, which my aesthetically trained eye immediately perceived, allowed them to move about with the aid of a single crutch. With it propped under their one arm, and hopping on their one leg, they could flit around with reasonable dexterity. If the absence of limbs had been vertical – if they'd lacked an arm and a leg on the same side of the body, say – getting about would have been much more difficult for them. That would have lessened my problem because I wouldn't have needed to fear that they could accost me or – horror of horrors – even touch me.

Now as they came closer, I saw that the father of the family wasn't intact either. He had no arms from the elbows down. He also lacked ears and a nose, which was only fair in a way, because what would he do without hands if he wanted to pick his nose or dig in his ear with a little finger? And was that a limp he had? His legs looked as if they'd been beaten into the shape of an X. Again, two diagonals, I noted. The children, as so often happens, combined the features of their father and mothers. They all looked the same: dark-skinned and dirty, with pale, gummed-up eyes. It would have been impossible to distinguish them if it had not been for their bodily imperfections.

Should I Stay or Should I Go, I thought, as this family of invalids shuffled towards me, accompanied by whooping and the rhythmical clacking of crutches. But I didn't take to my heels because just at that moment the writer in me awoke, after having lain dormant for years. Literature thrives on human misfortune, and the beggars in front of me were a prime example of the agony of existence. It occurred to me that if I couldn't squeeze a good story out of them, I'd never be able to write. Having now found a way to exploit them, I decided to spend a little longer in their company. Yet at the same time, I realised that they also had an idea or two about how to exploit me. Perhaps they'd decided to club me to death with their crutches and then eat me. A fatso like me would be food for them for a whole month, I worried. My body would never be found, if I was searched for at all. No-one saw me enter the car park, and no-one would ever think of looking for me here; my mind played over a paranoid scenario.

Fortunately, I found a way of giving them the slip. I scaled the fire-escape stairs up to the ventilation duct of the nuclear shelter. It was clear to me that those invalids would never be able to make it up here, and sure enough, the head of the family scrutinised the stairs, almost to the point of sniffing them like a dog. As I'd assumed, he concluded I was beyond their reach. He turned to the family and spread his arms – or what he had left of them – in a gesture of helplessness.

They all gathered beneath me and called out in one voice for alms, obviously without thinking for a second how pointless their demand was. I watched them from my vantage point like populist leaders behold the crowd from the balconies where they hold their speeches. The small children reached out their trembling little hands towards me. Only then did I notice that every hand had only three fingers. The Serbian three-finger salute, I thought to myself!

So I yelled down to them like Slobodan Milošević at one of his rallies in the nineties, 'I love you too!'

'We're hungry, give us alms!' called one of the one-armed women. 'Please ... May God grant you health,' said the other.

That cheered me up no end; a person afflicted by leprosy had just wished me good health!

'See, you're laughing,' said the head of the household, determined to seize on my good mood. 'Give us food and we'll make you laugh all night long.'

Ha, these weren't beggars but entertainers! The five grubby children had perhaps taken *The Jackson 5* as models. Since that was a respectable way of providing for oneself, I promised to throw them a few crumbs. I took a good swig from my bottle.

'If you want to eat, tell me about yourselves,' I proposed. And that they did.

They were originally from Kosovo. They'd had a hard time all their lives, the father emphasised, as if that didn't go without saying for every human being. 'Me and my two ladies went from town to town,' he explained. 'Then the children came along, three little angels,' he sighed wistfully.

'With swarthy faces,' I added with compassion.

He claimed that they'd worked hard but never earned enough for a house of their own. Therefore, they slept in caves. In a cavern near Prizren they came across a colony of lepers. They tried to flee, but the lepers blocked the exit with their bodies, a barrier more effective than electrified barbed wire. They let him go, but his wives and children were held hostage. Every day he had to bring the lepers food, he said. That went on for months. Then they were liberated by NATO, which was bombing Serbia at the time; it seems a pilot missed his target and his rocket hit the cave. They fled through the flames as the cave collapsed behind them.

A period of prosperity followed for the polygamous family. Infected with leprosy but as yet unaware of it, they roamed from village to village after the residents had fled to Albania to escape the Serbian army.

'The soldiers left us alone,' the paterfamilias said. 'We told them we're Balkan Egyptians,[1] and they had nothing against us. Nor we against them. And when they came in trucks and took away everything of value in the villages, there was still enough for us.'

But when the Serbian army withdrew and the Kosovar villagers returned to their ransacked homes, difficult times were in store for the family. Everyone beat them up and they were blamed for all ills, the head of the household complained. When irate villagers raped his wives and broke his legs with a pickaxe, they realised they'd better run for it. They ended up here in Ulcinj, and regretted it a hundred times. No-one gave them a lousy dinar here, he bellyached. It's as if the people here had no feelings. But the worst was yet to come...

'We have no education,' they told me. 'So how were we to know that we'd come down with leprosy too? We

---

1   *Albanian-speaking Romanies (Gypsies) who believe that their ancestors migrated from the Indian Subcontinent to Europe via Egypt.*

caught if from those miserable lepers in the cave.'

'When my missus came up with a lump on her back, I got worried and took her to see a doctor. And he called the police,' the head of the family said. 'Men with gas masks came, armed with hoses, and evacuated the dispensary. We and the doctor were quarantined. He was let out the next day when they established he wasn't infected, but we were held there for a few days more. And then one evening we were brought here to the abandoned car park. If we ever came out or so much as poked our noses out of the car park, we'd be killed, the police warned us. But I no longer had a nose then – it had fallen off all by itself.' He laughed heartily at the police's stupidity.

From then on, the years were filled with misery. Two more children were born, and they lost the odd arm and leg. But all in all they led a peaceful life, he said. The police's threat had been quite unnecessary; 'We're not going anywhere,' he emphasised.

'If anyone tries to drive us out of the car park, we'll fight for our right to stay,' the whole family chipped in.

The car park had become the home they'd been searching for all their lives. They claimed to have everything down there: food, a roof over their heads, and peace and quiet.

'In the world outside we get beaten up and abused, and we'd be strangers wherever we went. But down here we're masters of our own home,' the head of the family explained. 'Outside my children would be despised, but here they grow up surrounded by love. Outside they'd

grow up seeing others beat and humiliate me, while here
in the car park I can gain their respect. That's important
because I'm their father. We stay because we're happy
here,' he said, unaware that he'd just convincingly refuted
Tolstoy, who claimed that all happy families are happy in
the same way.

I have a vision, I wanted to tell them. I am a piper with a
funny Tyrolean cap, which Thomas Bernhard would find
laughable, and am dressed in green knickerbockers with
suspenders like Heidegger used to wear. I march along
blowing my pipe. And just as the rats faithfully followed
the Pied Piper of Hamelin, whom German towns hired
to rid them of the bright-eyed rodents, so the abandoned,
homeless and sick shall follow me. I play my pipe, and
the leprous beggars totter after me up the stairs, and we
leave the car park into the summer night full of neon
and lust. The music from my magic pipe needles its way
through the blaring bands on the café terraces and makes
it through to every old lady about to be poisoned by her
relatives so they can share out the inheritance; to every
child who will be suffocated by its mother in a shanty
on the outskirts and thrown into a stream clogged with
plastic bags and old umbrellas; to every AIDS-infected
young woman who trembles in her room, dreading the
moment when people will find out; to every raped boy; to
every alcoholic dying of liver cirrhosis down in the cellar,
banished and abandoned by his ex-wife and children
upstairs; to everyone on the verge of suicide, standing
on a rickety chair with a noose around their neck – my
music is like a waking hand which reaches out to all the

88

tuberculosed, the blind and deaf, the paraplegics and lepers. They are my army! Arrayed in a column behind me, they limp, lurch, stagger, crawl, drag their withered legs, and roll along in their wheelchairs. They follow my footsteps, just like the rats followed the Pied Piper. This is my grisly army beneath banners of blood-drenched bandages. Like avengers, we enter city after city and leave our mark in parliaments, malls, schools and hospitals. With every step we take we spread disease and disaster. We sneeze, pee, bleed, and leave bacilli on everything we touch. Wherever we go, we remake everything in our likeness, and all that is living falls before the contagion. Now they are all my soldiers. Faithfully they form a mighty column, and I think: *O children of the dark generations, silvery do shine the evil flowers of blood on our brows, and the cold moon in our broken eyes, o my blighted brethren!*

This is my grisly army, and there are ever more and more of us: all the beggars of Delhi, all the homeless of Brooklyn, all those who have grown up beneath Cairo and all the hungry of Kinshasa. Longer and ever longer is the column behind me, and the choir of a billion diseased voices, in unison, roars the cheerful refrain played by the pipe: *Death to Everyone is Gonna Come*. Here we are now on the sea shore, and here I am walking on water. *Death to Everyone* ... I play and mark time as I watch the cliffs over which my army, my grisly army, plunges into the sea and vanishes in the blue depths. I play faster and faster, now it is already *tempo furioso*: without a tear, without a scream, without regret and remorse, all that is mine falls to its death.

III

'Master?' I was roused from reflection by the father leper's rasping voice. 'Give us food now, we've done our part of the bargain.'

What can I give them when I've got nothing but whisky, I asked myself rhetorically. I took another swig and threw him the bottle.

'Don't overdo it with the fire water,' I was even bold enough to warn them.

As they were trying to bend over and pick up my Glenfiddich, I used the distraction to zip down the safety stairs. Just when I thought I'd gracefully backed out of things, albeit without saying goodbye, the greedy kid grabbed me by the trousers. I shot him a reproving look. He tried to hold me back with all the three fingers of one hand, while demanding alms with the open hand of the other. So I gave him a gentle kick in the stomach with the tip of my shoe, in a fatherly sort of way. I hardly touched him, but the little monster raised such a racket that his father and mothers, after examining him and establishing he was all right, headed off after me seeking revenge. 'Liar, bastard, scum!' I heard them fume as I ran for the exit.

It was three in the morning when I found myself in the world outside again. The mob of tourists was gradually dispersing.

I drove slowly. The roots of ruin can be seen in every

stone by the roadside if you care to look, if you only try to learn, I thought. The road I was driving along was the one the Montenegrin army climbed when it came to take Ulcinj from the Turks. Up in the clearing, where you can look out into the blue emptiness all the way across the Adriatic to Otranto on the one side, and down onto the plain of Štoj and the salt pans on the other, they clashed with a small Turkish unit. After that they advanced down through the streets of Ulcinj to the walls of the Old Town. But their attack was repulsed, and they let out their rage by burning down part of the town. It would later be rebuilt, and today the suburb is called *Nova Mahala* or New Quarter – talk about a euphemism! The wooden houses and hundreds of little bridges burned through until dawn, illuminating the path into the future for the people of Ulcinj.

When he finally captured Ulcinj, King Nicholas had a church built beneath the walls of the Old Town. They say that parts of the Cyclopean ramparts, thousands of years old, were used to build the church. Pieces of the damaged walls which had plunged down into the sea from the besiegers' cannonade during the siege were masoned into the church. Later, a new settlement was raised around the church. For that they levelled the Muslim cemetery where the people of Ulcinj had buried their dead for centuries; they knocked down the gravestones, threw them into the sea, stamped and trampled the ground, and built their houses there as if it was virgin land.

Where is there any chance of human happiness in

all this, I wondered. Amid the death, destruction and dispossession which had been present from the very beginning and would last until the end. It seemed impossible to find happiness, and I gave myself up to the satisfaction of moralising for a few moments, before stopping the car and parking in front of the wall surrounding the Orthodox church.

That was the closest I was going to get. The shortest route to the Old Town led through the courtyard of the church, but I never thought of going that way. If Catholicism enraged me and Judaism bored me, if I pitied Islam and disdained Protestantism, Orthodoxy filled me with sheer disgust. That's why, instead of going through the church's courtyard, I went the long way round, past overflowing garbage containers which the municipal services hadn't emptied for days. If I have to choose between the reek of rubbish and the stench of incense, I always choose the first. Rather dirty streets than seedy cassocks, I said to myself. If I'm stupid and desperate enough to seek salvation and place my hope in it, I'll search for it on the asphalt, certainly not before the altar. I choose the world the way it is rather than swallow the lies for the weak.

With these thoughts in my mind, I arrived at the gates of the Old Town. I could hear steps coming towards me along the dark street, and a man ran past me carrying what looked like a dog or a child in his arms. I caught a glimpse of his face and saw that his eyes were full of tears, while his contorted lips revealed the despair he felt. Behind him, like penguins bereft of any trace of amiability, there waddled several headscarved women in pantaloons. Not one of them was taller than five foot or weighed less than 160 pounds. They looked like pygmy sumo wrestlers. John Waters would have paid a fortune to have them in one of his films. These kerchiefed penguins shrieked unbearably. It was clear they were bemoaning something, but aren't we always doing that, and mostly bemoaning ourselves? Like grotesque performers, they tap-danced in their tiny wooden-soled slippers over the cobblestones worn smooth with time. Although they'd never realise it, time would render trivial every pain they'd ever felt and would make both them and whatever they were lamenting that night pass without a trace, like the wind blows through the desert.

I was heading for Terra Promessa, where I was a regular and could sit on the terrace and drink for hours. It was a nice bar with a perfect view of the sea where they played Johnny Cash and Merle Haggard: *some of the best that conservative America has produced*, the waiter once commented. He had a strange ideological profile I never quite understood.

'I travelled a lot when I was young. I was even at Woodstock,' he told me once. 'I was a liberal. But then I thought a lot and read a lot, and there you are – today I'm a conservative.'

That was unusual because people are normally conservative because they *don't* think or read.

'You do understand, of course, that any ideological definition is completely pointless,' I said to him. 'Accepting any idea simply means that we haven't yet thought about it enough, because everything becomes absolutely unacceptable as soon as we think twice about it. Do you realise how paltry your dispute with the leftists is?' I asked him. 'In trying to improve the world, you make life even harder for everyone. You enact laws and rules which make our already wretched existence even more miserable, and then you even fight wars, although that isn't so bad – fortunately people die in war, so those lucky beggars are at least put out of their misery. You do understand, of course, that you're all going to snuff it in the end. And what's more, it will be in despair. There won't be a single idea, song or slogan behind which you'll be able to hide from the fact that you're dying, that you don't know why you've lived or why you're dying, that you've never known what is good and what is evil, and that you've always only ever done evil, especially when you most firmly believed you were doing good. But that really doesn't matter because not only will the border between good and evil blur for you in the hour of your death, but you won't even be sure if good and evil exist at all, and you'll feel at your death that good and evil are just ideological constructs which were necessary to help you scrape through,' I told him.

He didn't answer, but he realised it was better to avoid conversing with me. Since then we've developed a wonderful relationship: he brings me my drink in silence, and I drink in silence. He exists solely as the one who serves, and I solely as the one who pays him for it. A whisky or two in the 'promised land', and then I'd drive home to bed, I thought.

But a foreboding that the future wasn't going to be so nice grew on me as I walked along the narrow lanes. The people I met on the way were shocked and emotional. Women were leaning on the windowsills and crying, while men stood in front of the houses and smoked in silence. I tried to make out what they were whispering about. I heard just one word of Albanian, a language I've never learnt although I've been immersed in it all my life. They repeated that one word, and it followed me like a hissing snake all the way to Terra Promessa. It slid after me down the dark alleys overgrown with ivy like a giant serpent bearing misfortune on its back. *Pus*, they said over and over again.

The bar was empty, and there was no music. I took that as final confirmation of my presentiment that some misfortune had struck. Misfortunes happen all the time – what else is there anyway? – but people only notice it on occasion. Usually they take all their life to realise that everything was misfortune, from their birth onwards. Admittedly, a certain subtlety is required to see a reason for sadness in the birth of a child. Therefore, people only show sorrow when misfortune takes a vulgar manifestation, like when an aeroplane crashes or miners are trapped underground. Then they turn off all music, which for them is a form of entertainment, despite the greatest value of music being that it is so lovely to mourn to.

The waiters stood at the bar, spreading their arms and shaking their heads in a demonstration of helplessness and disbelief. I cleared my throat several times in the hope of attracting their attention. They only came after I'd resorted to more radical methods: taking a crystal dish for ice from the next table and throwing it to the floor at their feet, where it smashed to smithereens and made it *crystal clear* to them that I was demanding my drink.

My conservative waiter explained to me the strange events I had witnessed that night. *Pus* is the Albanian word for well. A child had fallen into a well and died. But, strangely, the boy hadn't drowned. He fried to death.

In his sleep, the boy's father had heard someone lifting the lid of the well, one of many which residents of the Old Town still have in their courtyards like mementoes of a bygone age. Some thirsty tourist again, he thought, and turned his head to the other side of the pillow. Then he distinctly heard someone fall in, and squeals like those of a slaughtered animal came from that hole in the ground and woke up the whole neighbourhood. When they saw their son's footprints in front of the well, his mother fainted. His father took a long rake and managed to haul up the little charred body; the unfortunate boy was burnt beyond recognition. One bystander suggested lowering a bucket to see what could have burned the boy so quickly. It was brought up full of molten lava, caught fire and fell back into the well.

'But there's no volcano here, or at least there wasn't until now, so how's this possible?' the waiter marvelled. 'What's more, lava has also been found farther up the coast, at Mozura, and it looks like lava was the cause of the fire there. There was also lava at Velika Plaža beach, and the underbrush is still burning from it. I bet they'll find lava in Bratica, too. The fire brigade can't get at it there. The road to Bar is cut off and the whole town surrounded by flames. What if a hidden volcano beneath Ulcinj explodes tonight?' the waiter asked. 'What will happen to us then?'

I paid up and hurriedly fled the scene because his story contained an apocalyptic tone I found particularly unnerving. But we flee in vain. Misfortune comes in bunches, like poisonous flowers or bombs dropped to destroy the last sanctuary of our solitude and calm. I escaped the waiter only to run into Dirty Djuro again, for the second time that night. I'd made it to the gate of the Old Town when he intercepted me like a jet fighter invisible to my radar.

'My friend, let me take you to *Servantes*. My daughters are doing a dance number there,' he said.

Servantes, as I was to learn, was a newly opened cabaret-bar on the Slave Market in the Old Town. Here I always used to come across panting, sweaty tourists photographing the slave cages, which gape shamefully empty today although the world is full of people who ought to be locked up. I've always appreciated that place as one of the few surviving pieces of evidence that the town I live in belongs to Western civilisation. The Ulcinj corsairs were once the scourge of the coastal towns all the way north to Istria. The Ottoman Empire sank their fleet in Valdanos Bay in the mid eighteenth century after the corsair leaders refused obedience to the Sultan. In any case, the corsairs abducted people throughout the Mediterranean and sold them here at their Slave Market. The documents bearing witness to this lead us to believe that Ulcinj's Slave Market was famous far and wide. The slaves who changed hands here were taken all the way to Constantinople in the east and Vienna in the west. Historical sources which don't seem particularly reliable allege that the man who later wrote *Don Quixote* was also brought here, sun-parched and fettered, and sold. Inspired by the knowledge that the inhabitants of Ulcinj had enslaved Miguel Cervantes, which was undoubtedly their greatest contribution to world culture, I imagined today's Slave Market as the perfect venue for an artistic event; a place where writers would read from their oeuvre and then be auctioned off to the literature lover who bid the highest. After paying an adequate fee to the publisher, readers would be allowed to take a wet whip and flog a writer they particularly hated. Or loved. Ladies who dreamed of having children who'd become artists could be impregnated by gifted authors. Such a concept would create the opportunity for countless debates about the social role of writers, freedom of artistic expression and the commodification of literature.

But other art forms were in demand in Servantes, I thought to myself as Djuro led me into the smoky premises illuminated by green and red neon lights. His daughters were doing a striptease on an improvised stage in the centre.

Located behind the Romanesque church, which had been converted first into a mosque and then into a museum, a dilapidated stone house had been made into a brothel and named after the famous writer. The people of Ulcinj gave him no peace even in death. Djuro had announced that the programme would be spectacular. But his daughters had problems with the choreography, to put it kindly. Their movements were devoid of the slightest trace of elegance, and they tried to tie them into something which could only be called 'erotic dance' with a lethal dose of sarcasm.

Through the thicket of *oohs* and *ahs* accompanying this performance I heard a deep male voice addressing the barman: 'A double pepper vodka for me, and a double of your best whisky for my friend here.' I looked for the owner of that impressive voice: he was an elderly, grey-haired man in a fine jute suit with a neatly trimmed beard, a topi above a high forehead, and keen eyes.

We exchanged several polite sentences. That was the least I could do for a man who'd bought me a drink. He was, as people like to say, a man of the world: an old-school gentleman with good manners and an education which can only be provided by classical lyceums and top-notch European universities. Only when you finally meet someone with good manners do you realise why they're so important – they allow you to communicate with others without getting too close to them. Good manners can help you to keep at a hygienic distance from people, which is impossible to maintain when evil fate forces us into contact with primitives who constantly desire to become intimate with us and are offended when they learn that we don't want any proximity.

'Is this your first time in Ulcinj?' I asked him.

'Not exactly', he replied. 'It would be truer to say I've been here all along.'

'That amazes me,' I said. 'This is a small town where everyone knows everyone else, and I don't remember having met you before.'

'You know, what I really meant is that I feel at home everywhere, metaphorically speaking,' the stranger remarked.

'Truly cosmopolitan spirits are rare today,' I said, and drained my glass. 'People have everything within arm's reach, the world is at their feet and all knowledge at their fingertips, but the world is still ruled by ignorance and prejudice.'

'You're quite right,' the old man agreed. 'It's the same with me: nothing vexes me more than prejudice. You just can't explain things to some people because prejudice makes them blind and deaf. I have always most highly prized openness for new ideas and a freedom of mind. Those who have that are my people,' he averred, rapping his knuckles on the bar.

After a brief pause he continued, 'My dear Sir, although we've only just met I feel I've known you all my life – you're a man of style, that's clear as soon as anyone sees you.'

'The same could be said of you,' I returned the compliment.

'Yes, yes,' he muttered, 'I guess people have accused me of many things, but no-one has challenged my style. Therefore, I say to you, because you'll understand me:

this little orgy behind us here will come to a bad end,' he said with confidence and conviction. 'That's the problem with people – their lack of style. Their inability to transcend their limitations. And so every attempt to rise above oneself ends in obscenity; the more ambitious the attempt, the greater the obscenity.'

There was nothing to add to his words. It's rare to encounter a kindred soul. Sophisticated people are condemned to solitude. Therefore, when we meet a like-minded person, we should make sure to enjoy their company. Determined to chat a little longer with the old man, I ordered another round of drinks.

Then Samir the Wahabi strode into the premises. Servantes really brought out his messianic syndrome. He cursed the naked girls and the men who were watching them.

'Go home to your wives,' he yelled. 'God will punish you all and scorch you with His wrath.'

That was all Samir managed to say before someone hit him and he fell to the floor. Diligent feet kicked him and a barrage of fists found their mark. He was carried out of the café, covered in blood, and thrown into the nearby bushes.

'If you ask me, he came to grief because he moralised,' I said to the old man. 'He came at a bad time and said the wrong things. It's as simple as that. To go into a brothel and lecture a pack of sex-hungry men about God and punishment is bound to end badly.'

'Why do they do that, I ask you?' the old man growled and banged his fist on the bar. 'Why do they confound the already hopeless tangle of their lives with things like morality, philosophy and religion? Why don't they ever choose the simpler way when it's so obvious? And why the remorse when they do choose a path? All this and the whole world is just a conspiracy of fools, my dear fellow. It's all been devised to make life miserable for us people with spirit. Couldn't some good Gypsy ensemble have played here tonight instead? Couldn't people have sat here in peace and drank some of the quality local wines? I beg your pardon, a man of taste will refuse wine – whisky then. Couldn't they have served a single malt from the Scottish Highlands? Couldn't they have all been contented tonight? But no! This is just an example of how easy it is for everything to fall apart. And where has this got us to, I ask you? Instead of whisky, blood flows – not that I have anything against it. But where there's blood, there's wine. That short trajectory from blood to wine contains all the lies of this world, all that makes people's lives miserable. Turn blood into wine and you've turned the world into a hell where they drown people in cauldrons of seething guilt and roast them on the pyre of illusions – a hell for those condemned to eternally repeat one and the same question: why?

'I feel we've got to know one another pretty well. Instead of music, we have the tears of a martyr – a fool, to be frank, who suffered due to his own arrogance. That's how things go, *my son*,' he said. Seizing my hand in his torrid fist, he intoned: 'There are still so many things I have to say to you, *my son*.'

'Old fool!,' I thought. He started off well, in fact he

did brilliantly, but now he's gone and called me *son*. If we continue the conversation it will turn out that I remind him of a son he lost long ago, some sad story about losing a beloved child will pop up like a zombie, and everything will end up in pathos, cheap advice and tears. I'll have to put him in his place, I thought. That will offend the old man, but I have no choice.

'Our conversation is over. Good night to you,' I said and headed for the door.

'You know, of course, that it won't be as easy as that. Let me assure you that you don't really want to leave me, *my son*,' he replied, maliciously accentuating those last two words. 'Let me tell you a few interesting things about you. Is it not true that your wife has left you, not one day ago? I have your attention now, don't I? The wife who you loved has left you. They say: *love*, but what does that mean other than *to suffer when you lose it?* You loved her, and you lost her. So it seems. But *on second thought*, as you like to say, you'll realise that you didn't lose her, nor could you have, because you never owned her. She was never *yours*. You don't *have* other people, just as they don't *have* you. You live separate lives. Sometimes people are useful to you, like when you take what you need from a toolbox. Other times they're an obstacle to be avoided, and sometimes removed. Ultimately, you're left to your own devices in an extremely hostile environment, where everything that exists is there to make your life difficult and ultimately destroy you.

'*I know all that*, you'll say. Yes, you did, and yet you got married although you knew better,' the old man said.

'I can just see the two of you: it's quite plain that you take devotion for love and don't discern the difference between tolerance and love. You say to yourself: I love her, but actually you only just put up with her. You think: I put up with her because I love her, and love means denial. That explains everything, you think. But why then do you get up every morning before dawn, open the bedroom door a crack to check she's sleeping, and sit down at the computer? Why then do you search for pornography on the internet and spend those early-morning hours, those precious moments of solitude, masturbating? Then regret befalls you, or is it that you're worried she'll discover your dirty little habit? You take your hands off *Richard*, so to speak, and shun the computer, but you still can't sleep. There's no sleep for you since she's lain in your bed. You wake every morning at the same time. Three minutes past three, it says on the clock, whose red numbers blink on the shelf above your head. You're woken by strange noises. You hold your breath to try and hear them better, you listen hard, but you can't tell where the noises are coming from. Sometimes you think you hear footsteps outside the window. Or is that the rustling of sheets from the kitchen – you imagine they're white and hover over the table, borne on a wind which opens the window and rushes into the room. At other times you're sure that someone, or *something*, is up in the roof; that it scratches its nails on the plaster and gnaws at the rafters; and that that someone or *something* will keep maltreating you until you lose your mind. You get up and search the house, trying not to wake her. She mustn't find out, you think: *that* would be too much for her. You search the house but find nothing.

'*I love her*, you think now as you sit in the car, staring at the gate of the clinic and waiting for her to come out, purged of your child. But when she lowered her head onto your lap, as helpless as a broken, golden doe; when she lay on your legs, blinked with tears in her eyes and fearfully said *I'm pregnant*; when you, at those words, pushed her aside and brutally shouted *What?*; when she doubled up in the armchair, buried her face in her hands and cried; when you told her you could put up with her but not a child, and she had to get rid of it straight away; when you told her a child would eat away your existence like a brood of rats and would kill you, you finished what she'd begun; when you told her that you're not capable of devoting a single shred of attention to the child and that you already have a child – her – and she must therefore choose between you and the child; when all of that was in the air you actually wondered: *Do I love you?*

'And before she could even think things over you threw her into the car and drove her to the clinic. She'd leaned her head against your shoulder and nestled up to you, but you didn't say a word. You refused so much as to look at her. Was her transgression so huge that not even a love like yours could brook it? Was her pregnancy too great a transgression to forgive? You harshly threw her off you, onto the seat beside you; then you threw her into the car like a sackful of rubbish; soon you cast her out in front of the clinic as if it was a rubbish container. She emerged from there an hour later, bent and black, a shadow of the person you *loved*.

'When she came to her senses in the morning and realised what she'd done, and above all what you'd done to her, she left you. "Everything I thought I had to sacrifice the child for is gone. Everything I discarded the child for so I could keep you no longer exists. So everything that was a reason to stay with you is now a reason to leave you. My love for you is *aborted*," she said.

'That's why I ask you: why are you leaving me and where are you going? Haven't you decided to tread the so-called path of virtue?' the old man asked. 'But where does it lead? And even if you lived the life of a righteous man and arrived at the wisdom they preach, what would await you in the hour of your death? What would you think of when your soul, that most precious of all things, was separating from the body? I'll tell you: you'd feel only fear of what lies ahead. Only fear and remorse, as long as your wisdom and righteousness were guiding you. At the peak of their wisdom and hour of their death, people repent every moment they've lived, except those where they suffered the most. You can arrive at that wisdom, and it will only reward you with more suffering. I knew a man who said: W*hen I'm desperate, I'm strong*. Is that a wise man or a saint, as some may call him, or is he simply crazy?

'Finally, I appeal to your humanity,' he said. 'Stay here with me. In the name of compassion. Have pity on the poor old man now, since you didn't pity your mother.

You may have let your mother die in excruciating pain, you may have left her, but don't leave this old man. You may have been deaf to her words when she begged you to kill her, but don't be blind and deaf to me,' he pleaded.

Tired, angry and nauseated, as if I couldn't live a moment longer, I closed my eyes.

I woke beneath the walls of the Old Town. I must have stumbled on the way home and fallen asleep there.

I looked around me. It was first light. The sun was slowly rising, but its terrible heat wouldn't unfold until later. The streets were empty and there was no-one to offend my retina. I'd always imagined the empty town as a perfect backdrop for my life. At dawn, the colossal crime machine is still warming up. The mighty engine doesn't start with a rumble and a whistle until everyone has done their morning toilet, had their first coffee, kissed their daughters in their beds, said goodbye to their families and gone down to the street, that conveyor belt for the production of abominations. At dawn the world seems least defiled – only then is it tolerable. All the sordidness of the day has still to happen. I remembered the old hi-fi my father used to play his classical-music cassettes on when I was a child. Sometimes I'd press the *PAUSE* button, and he'd come in from the kitchen and start the tape again. Now is that moment between me and my father, I thought – the moment after I'd pressed *PAUSE* on the matrix of the world and before the tape started turning again. I inhaled deeply and closed my eyes, determined to imbibe some of the morning's silver-blue silence.

Suddenly I knew that the morning had died and everything had started again. The machine was set in motion: I heard the rushing sound of cars in the street and passers-by calling out to one another. As if a dyke had burst, thousands of people plunged down towards the town from the surrounding hills and it vanished beneath a flood of human bodies. Cheap flip-flops fluttered like the wings of bats. Bony feet with toes and nails now covered the asphalt, the façades were wrapped in human skin, and gouged-out eyes blinked in place of traffic lights and public lighting. People literally trampled one another. They'll all pour into the sea, I thought. Only the roofs of houses could still be seen above the torrent of *humanity* spewing through the town.

I ran for the pavement, determined to flee before the masses swept me away. But when I tried to look at my face in a nearby shop window, all I could see was the river of nameless people behind me.

Suddenly I heard the voice of a boy or a girl, I know not which, coming from the neighbouring house, chanting over and over again, 'Pick it up, read it. Pick it up, read it.' Immediately I ceased weeping and began most earnestly to think whether it was usual for children in some kind of game to sing such a song, but I could not remember ever having heard the like.

I looked into the vortex of sunburnt and peeling human bodies behind me and thought of that voice and its ethereal song. Then it became clear to me: I've finally gone under in the sea of *them*, I thought. Finally, I can see no more difference between myself and *them*. I was drowning, but it wasn't the feeling of horror I'd always expected it to be. Instead, I felt relief. I had to reach the point where I could no longer see myself; I had to disappear for myself so I could finally feel relief.

We see so much sadness around us every day. We see it, and yet we don't recognise it, I thought. To loathe people means not to understand anything, and even worse: to not understand them properly. Loathing is nothing but superficiality at its worst – when superficiality is fortified by conceitedness. We loathe people because we think we see them the way they are. We're proud of our loathing and work on it assiduously, cultivating it like a rare plant.

But all that is a lie. We hate people because we don't understand anything, and that lack of understanding is all the more profound because we think we do understand. We find everything around us grotesque, but actually it's only we who are grotesque – we, the seekers of the grotesque. That's how we see things before we understand. And when we do, we realise that everything is just endlessly sad, including us and everyone else. There's nothing more to understand. There's just that sea of sadness which you cannot sail and cannot walk on; there's no room for miracles here. Just that sea of sadness, in which we drown. We thrash about with our arms and legs, sometimes managing to lift our head above the surface in our panic, and sometimes we even think we're going to come through. But how wrong we are. In the end we drown, like all others before us have and all others after us will, I said to myself. We drown, the sadness swallows us up and closes over us as if we'd never existed, and only when we stop struggling and end our ridiculous attempts at resistance do we find relief. We need to go the whole path from repulsion to pity, from rejection to acceptance. We have to drown to finally find relief.

The man who brought me my father's goats was unhappy. If you saw him, you'd say: what an idiot. And yet how much wisdom was needed to come up to me – someone like me – and say *You're a good man*. How much wisdom, or whatever it was, doesn't matter in the end; he was able to comprehend another's despair, and nothing else counted. He saw how unhappy I was. Only a fool could fail to see how unhappy Uroš was. Or the family of lepers in the car park. How unhappy Djuro's daughters were, and Djuro himself, I thought. And then I desired to tell them that. I felt a need to tell them that I hadn't seen it before but that I saw it now. I got into the car and sped off to find them.

I had to see the lepers urgently. I ran down the stairs into the underground car park and started calling them right from the top. 'Hey, lepers!' I shouted. I rushed along the dark terraces of the car park and then went down as far as the nuclear shelter, hoping to find them where I'd left them. But I found no trace of them. They've probably fled into some dark nook and are now looking at me in fear, determined to stay hidden, I thought. 'I come as a friend,' I yelled, trying to get them to come out. I wanted to offer them money and medicine for their ailments. *And with medicine in hand he descended among the lepers*, I laughed in desperation.

Back to the car, then straight to Djuro's flat. I dashed to the cellar door and hammered at it. There was no reply, not even from Djuro's wife who I imagined had to be home. I put my ear to the door and listened for the crying of Djuro's brats. Instead I heard the old woman from the floor above cursing and threatening to call the police if I didn't go away immediately. It wouldn't have worked anyway, I reflected as I was leaving. I'd have gone up to Tanja, handed her the money and said: *This is all for you, I only ask that you leave your father – that you go away and try to save your life, and thus save and justify mine.* But after all that she would just have told me that she couldn't. She'd never leave because she loved her father.

***

I hadn't set foot in my father's house or spoken a word with him since my mother's death. In fact, I couldn't remember when I'd last seen him. How long had it been since I'd last looked from my terrace, like the balcony of a theatre, and seen my father sitting in his armchair out the front of his house? He used to sit there for hours and would stay there when night fell, motionless, staring at Uncle's hill, with Saint Augustine's *Confessions* on his lap.

That morning I felt the urge to see him. There were so many things I had to say to him and so much we had to discuss. I knew that sooner or later we'd have to do it, so why not straight away? I knocked resolutely on his door, ready to face the scathing indifference he'd receive me with. And when he didn't answer, I thought he must be sleeping, because it was still early. So I went round the back of the house to the summer kitchen, where my mother used to make dinner for the guests who dropped in less and less over time. My father, and then all of us, withdrew into ourselves, until there was no-one to visit us any more. The key hung on a hook in the stone wall above the sink as it always had.

I entered the dark hall. All the blinds were closed and light only made it in through the holes in the roof, which my father probably hadn't felt like mending. I tried to turn on the light, but there was no electricity. It was easy to imagine that my father didn't care about that – he probably didn't even open up when the debt collectors rang and didn't want to go into town to pay the light bill even after they'd finally disconnected him.

I opened the door of the main bedroom just a crack. The sheets and blankets on my parents' double bed were smooth and tucked in neatly. It was clear that no-one had lain in that bed since my mother last straightened up the house, that morning when she was taken to the hospital in Podgorica to die. My father must be sleeping in my room, I thought. But my room was locked. I called him and banged on that door I grew up behind, but there was no reply.

I looked for him in the bathroom, too. Water was dripping from the tap above the bath. I tried to turn it off, but it was no use: the rusty thing would keep on dripping until someone replaced it. I heard a swarm of flies buzzing above the toilet bowl, which stank terribly. The bath was covered in brown, slimy layers of filth.

The house looked as if no-one had lived in it for years. It was the chef-d'oeuvre of my father's ascetic concept, a way of life he adopted in his old age which involved renouncing anything that demanded the slightest effort.

It was clear that no-one had cleaned the house since my mother died. Tapestries of spiderwebs stretched from one end of the living room to the other. Half a loaf of bread lay on the kitchen table, mouldy green and as hard as stone. Beside it stood a half-drunk bottle of wine, now vinegar, and everything lay under two fingers of dust, like a shroud. On my father's desk, draped with a sheet on which the damp had traced dark spots, stood the ancient *His Master's Voice* gramophone. Solid mahogany with a huge brass horn. It was a present I gave him, a valuable acquisition from my

Year 12 excursion to Florence. When I returned, I had triumphantly presented him with several Bach records and the gramophone.

'It was made in 1933, and its first owner was a German industrialist who committed suicide a few years later,' I told him, repeating what I'd been told in the antique shop. 'His name is engraved in gold on the back, *Leopold Kleist*, but that's not why I bought it. You see, Leopold Kleist married a girl who was a direct descendant of Bach's – his great-great-granddaughter, so to speak. This was her gramophone and she listened to the music of her ancestor on it,' I said.

That was a lie, and the whole story was a device of the cunning Italian trader. But my father believed it because he needed to believe. He just looked at me with his eternally sad eyes. He didn't hug me or say thank you. He didn't have to: I knew how much the present meant to him.

Only then did I notice that all the bookshelves in my father's study were bare. Where had all those books gone? I gazed in puzzlement at the emptiness of the library he'd assembled throughout his life. All four walls of the room had once been covered with books, almost like wallpaper. 'Here we're protected from the world by an armour of knowledge,' my father used to say. Now the shelves were bare save for dead flies and rat droppings. All that was left were seven solidly bound red volumes on one of the lower shelves. I remembered the angelic voice singing, *Pick it up, read it. Pick it up, read it.* I lowered the tomes onto the desk with a thump, and through the cloud of dust that rose I saw that I'd just discovered my father's diaries.

Before I opened the blinds and light flooded into the house; before a Bach record crackled on the gramophone; before I went out onto the terrace and sat in my father's wicker armchair; before I glanced at Uncle's scorched hill, above which smoke was still rising; before I heard the bleating of goats in the courtyard; before I managed to calm down and before I thought everything now seemed quite acceptable – before all of that I took my father's diaries off the shelf, laid them on the desk and opened them, and with a start I became aware of the word which the man had pondered all this time; the word which had been wholly on his mind and hounded him. With a tremendous sense of fear which nearly destroyed me, I read what my father had written trance-like, in a shaky hand like a cardiogram, every day of the last years of his life; like a grisly army with its banners, a single word stretched in a column from line to line, from page to page, from one volume to the next, and from the first to the last – just one word: son.

Soundtrack for *THE SON*

1. MONO – *Moonlight*
2. JESSE SYKES AND THE SWEET HEREAFTER
   – *Reckless Burning*
3. GRAVENHURST – *Animals*
4. NOIR DÉSIR – *Le vent nous portera*
5. SIGUR RÓS – *8*
6. SONIC YOUTH – *Tunic (Song For Karen)*
7. INTERPOL – *Leif Erikson*
8. STEVE EARLE – *John Walker's Blues*
9. BONNIE PRINCE BILLY – *Death To Everyone*
10. THE WORKHOUSE – *Peacon*
11. J.S. BACH – *Suite No. 3: Air*
12. AMANDINE – *For All The Marbles*
13. BAND OF HORSES – *St. Augustine*

Quotations:

Georg Trakl on p. XX [at beginning]: *Georg Trakl: Poems and Prose. A Bilingual Edition*, Northwestern University Press 2005, trans. Alexander Stillmark

Thomas Bernhard on p. XX [at beginning]: *Gathering Evidence: A Memoir* by Thomas Bernhard, Vintage 2003, trans. David McLintock

St Augustine's *Confessions* on p. XX [to locate the page enter "*Suddenly I heard the voice*"] (trans. Albert C. Outler): www.ccel.org/ccel/augustine/confessions.xi.html. Retrieved 18 June 2013

The Son comes to you from Istros Books: a boutique publisher of quality literature in translation from South East Europe. If you have enjoyed this book, then perhaps you would like the others in our series:
Best Balkan Books 2013
Subscribe to all 4 books for only £28 directly at
www.istrosbooks.com

Sun Alley by Cecilia Ștefanescu (Romania)
A tender and magical love-affair between two children in the 1980s which is re-kindled in adulthood. Told through the eyes of a 12-year-old boy with a strange ability to see the future.
ISBN: 9781908236067, published: APRIL 2013

The Fairground Magician by Jelena Lengold (Serbia)
'Fairground Magician is a wonderful collection of short stories. Sensuous, charming, witty and urbane, Jelena Lengold's stories of complex relationships and passions are both highly literary and highly readable...'
Vesna Goldsworthy, author of *Chernobyl Strawberries*
Winner of the European Prize for Literature 2011
ISBN: 978-1-908236-10-4, published: SEPT2013

Ekaterini by Marija Knežević (Serbia)
'Between the scents of oranges and lemons, mixed with the sea breeze, the individual biography is played out against the larger picture of war." Eva Zonenberg-
Poet & author of *The Moment of Delight*
ISBN: 978-1-908236-13-5 , published: OCT 2013